C000052248

THE LYING DUTCHMAN

Master Mercurius Mysteries
Book Six

Graham Brack

SAPERE
BOOKS

THE LYING
DUTCHMAN

Published by Sapere Books.

20 Windermere Drive, Leeds, England, LS17 7UZ,
United Kingdom

saperebooks.com

Copyright © Graham Brack, 2022

Graham Brack has asserted his right to be identified as the
author of this work.

All rights reserved.

No part of this publication may be reproduced, stored in any
retrieval system, or transmitted, in any form, or by any means,
electronic, mechanical, photocopying, recording, or otherwise,
without the prior written permission of the publishers.

This book is a work of fiction. Names, characters, businesses,
organisations, places and events, other than those clearly in the
public domain, are either the product of the author's
imagination, or are used fictitiously.

Any resemblances to actual persons, living or dead, events or
locales are purely coincidental.

ISBN: 978-1-80055-645-4

PROLOGUE

Those who have followed my memoirs thus far have my thanks. Despite the pig's ear that my clerk Van der Meer has managed to make of taking my dictation, I am pleased that I have been able to set down some of my adventures before my inevitable death, which I hope to fend off for a while yet because I still have some tales to relate, not to mention completing the second volume of my series "Concerning the metaethics of St Thomas Aquinas and their relation to moral philosophy, with some notes on the proper Christian consideration of Aristotelian eudaimonism". Admittedly that series is not selling quite so well as my memoirs, but I have not done a lifetime's research for nothing, so I am determined to use it.

Old age affects men in various ways. God be thanked, my brain is unaffected. I wish I could say the same for my bladder. How I miss the days when I could pee when I wanted, where I wanted and in the direction I wanted! I am over eighty years old, and I still have most of my teeth, and if writing fatigues me at least I can still read. Van der Meer, on the other hand, despite being considerably younger, seems to be hard of hearing. He makes mistakes when I dictate to him. He claims that this is because I mumble, but I do nothing of the sort.

I find it harder to get to my favourite inn on the Langebrug these days, particularly if the paths are icy. Occasionally I send one of the kitchen boys to fetch me a jug of their ale for old times' sake, and in good weather I walk there and sit in my old place and think about the men I used to see there, now all gone, I fear. There is a loneliness to growing old, as your circle of acquaintances dwindles, and I remember what my dear grandmother used to say in her old age; there is no joy in being the last hen in the coop.

Fortunately I have my memories, and you shall have them too. A while ago one of the students here in Leiden who had read these volumes remarked to me that he had no idea I had played so great a part in Dutch life, because I wasn't mentioned in any of the standard histories; to which I replied that of course I wasn't, because I hadn't written my memoirs when they were compiled. It is not that I am proud — after all, it's the tallest ear of wheat in the field that is harvested first — but one must set the record straight.

Besides which, I have some particularly salacious gossip about a certain German bishop and his "niece" that I must try to work in somewhere. It has nothing to do with my story but that sort of thing keeps Van der Meer alert.

I hope you enjoy this tale. If you don't, it doesn't matter, because you've paid for the book anyway.

Leiden, St Bruno's Day, 1721

CHAPTER ONE

I don't know how many of my readers have ever seen a thing called a newspaper. The idea behind one of these is that someone has correspondents around the world who send him information which he then collects and has printed on a large sheet or two of paper and sells. It is quite an efficient way of getting news, so long as the correspondents are telling the truth and not just relating tittle-tattle.

Most of these publications are quite short-lived, but good ones are able to charge enough to pay their correspondents properly and therefore have more reliable intelligence for which some people are prepared to pay, though they are quite expensive. There are, for example, merchants who want to know what ships have arrived and departed. As a result, coffee and tea houses buy a copy of a newspaper for their customers to read. It is a way of encouraging customers to resort there.

This has not really caught on in Leiden, largely because we aren't very interested in what is happening anywhere else. We are, of course, deeply fascinated in what is going on in our city, the difficulty being that those who would buy the newspaper are the very people whose doings are likely to feature in it, not necessarily to their advantage, so there is no local newspaper here. However, occasionally a passing traveller will leave a newspaper at the inn, which is how I came to be reading the *Weekly Haarlem Courant* in early 1685 and thus discovered that King Charles II of England was dead.

This was simultaneously a great shock and no surprise at all. A shock, because he was only fifty-four years old, or, to put it another way, eight years older than me; no surprise, because if you had seen the sort of life he led it was astonishing that he had survived this long. He had at least a dozen illegitimate children and probably fourteen or fifteen mistresses, not to mention the scores of women of whom he had casual carnal knowledge over the years. He kept irregular hours and drank more than was good for him. He certainly suffered from gout as I had seen when I met him during a little trip to London of which I have previously written and which I do not choose to recall again. I still have cold sweats when I recall how close I came to having my throat cut on that occasion.

If the newspaper account was to be believed, Charles was not feeling well on Sunday and went for a carriage ride rather than taking his beloved dogs for a walk. Those dogs were a great nuisance about the palace; it was a large building with rambling corridors and even if the animals were sufficiently trained to want to go outside to make their mess, it was too far for them to make it in time, so as you walked through Whitehall Palace it was as well to watch where you were stepping.

It seems that Charles woke around seven o'clock on Monday morning and emitted a terrible cry before sinking back into his pillows and starting to convulse. Over the next few days he suffered very much, not just because of his illness, but because of the treatment given him by his doctors. He was repeatedly bled, given enemas and emetics and blistered with hot poultices applied to his skin. My colleagues in the Faculty of Medicine here told me that this was all unexceptionable and in line with the best medical practice; to which my answer is that there must be a very fine line between being a physician and being a torturer. Anyway, Charles finally died on the Friday morning, and news of this had just reached Haarlem when the newspaper was published.

I wondered idly whether our Stadhouder, William of Orange knew this. The chances are that our Ambassador in London would have written to tell William as a matter of urgency, because William would be affected by the change of monarch.

Trying to explain Charles' family tree is complicated, but this story won't make much sense unless I do. William's mother was Charles' sister. But it doesn't end there. Charles had no legitimate children, so the throne passed to his younger brother, James, Duke of York, who was therefore William's uncle; but because William had married James' daughter Mary he was also James' son-in-law.

Charles and William were both Protestants, though Charles was believed to have Catholic sympathies, but James had gone the whole hog and converted. Not only that, but he was an ardent Francophile. Charles had come to realise that the British people would not stand for a pro-French, pro-Catholic policy, and had therefore married Mary to William as the best guarantee that, even if James succeeded, the throne would revert to a Protestant thereafter. James had, I am told, some excellent qualities, among them personal bravery, but extreme intelligence was not one of them. Their father, Charles I, had believed in the Divine Right of Kings, that kings are appointed by God and answerable only to Him, and that, broadly speaking, a king could do what he wanted without question. This had ended badly when his own parliament cut his head off. You might have thought that this would have given James pause for thought, but as I said, if brains were candles you would barely have seen a flicker behind his eyes.

Anyway, as a result of the story in the newspaper James was now King, and it remained to be seen what sort of success he could make of it. If I were a betting man, which I am not, I would not have bet a bent duit on his success, but I comforted myself with the thought that I was not in England and had no plans ever to be so again. One trip to that ungodly place in a lifetime was enough for any man. It wasn't quite as awful as France, but there wasn't much in it, and the food was better in Troyes.

William's interest was that his wife was next in line to the English throne, and since a man and his wife are one in the eyes of the church, to William that meant that he was shortly to be king. After all, James was fifty-one years old, his brother and sister had died young, and although he had a younger second wife, they had been married for over eleven years without producing a living child.

Have you noticed that sometimes people's precautions bring about the very thing that they were worried about? Charles had an illegitimate son, also called James, who was Duke of Monmouth, and a staunch Protestant. I had met him at The Hague the previous year, where he was in exile and trying to solicit William's help to claim the throne if and when Charles died. So far William had avoided committing himself, but now he would have to make a decision.

A group of plotters in England had decided not to wait for Charles to die, but planned to give him some encouragement by kidnapping the King and his brother when they went to some horse races and killing them both before putting Monmouth on the throne. It all went wrong, and, even worse from the plotters' point of view, James received a lot of public sympathy that he had been the subject of such a foul design. He was in the unusual position of being popular. As a result, it was by no means sure that the English were very exercised one way or the other about their King's religion.

Now, I happened to know, having spoken to Princess Mary during one of William's "little jobs" that he liked to impose on me, that William had no intention of helping Monmouth because if Monmouth took the throne, Mary (and therefore William) would never occupy it. On the other hand, he didn't want to upset Protestant sentiment by openly opposing Monmouth's plan. He therefore found himself pursuing a devious policy in which he gave Monmouth every kind of assistance short of actual help. If Monmouth asked for money, he got it, but never quite enough; William let him recruit in the United Provinces but told important people not to sign up; and, most crucially of all, William sent the British troops stationed on our soil back to England without waiting to be asked.

We had some kind of treaty which placed British troops at William's disposal but on the understanding that King Charles could have them back whenever he needed them. By sending some back, William was giving Charles a coded warning that he might need them; and although Charles railed against William for giving shelter and support to his enemies, he quite liked the arrangement because he knew that William would feed him intelligence like a good nephew. William and Charles were not close; Charles liked wine, women and song, whereas William liked fighting, money and prayer, leading Charles to describe his nephew as the dullest youth in Christendom. However, you could rely on William to know where his interests lay, and at present they lay firmly with keeping Charles or James on the throne and keeping Monmouth off it.

While I had no doubt that William liked James even less than he liked Charles, he must have been relieved that James had, it seemed, succeeded to the throne of Great Britain without any drama or upset.

I returned the newspaper to the landlord and wrapped myself up well before venturing out to make the journey home. While it was not nearly as cold as the previous winter had been — how could it? — it was still very nippy when the wind whistled along the canals. It seems to funnel between the buildings somehow, and when there is a northerly wind it blows straight down the Rapenburg past the Academy building with barely anything to interrupt its flow.

Having arrived at the University I was standing just inside the door shaking off the rain and trying to unfasten my cloak when I was called by a very recognisable voice.

'Mercurius! May I have the pleasure of an interview? Now!'

I glanced up to the top of the staircase and, as I had expected, found myself looking at Professor Lucas Schacht, Professor of Medicine and Rector Magnificus of the University. Schacht was a muscular man with the most luxurious long brown hair. I wanted to ask him what pomade or dressing he used to make it so glossy, for many a maid would have been jealous of its sheen. He wore, as always, a crisp white jabot at his neck. He must have been responsible for the bulk of the University's starch bill, because it was always magnificently pressed.

Schacht was a man known for plain speaking. When he gave a diagnosis, he did not dress it up with fine words or circumlocutions. It must be mildly disconcerting when you go to a doctor with what you think is a mild indigestion only to be asked "Have you made your peace with God?" I found myself hoping that he had not diagnosed something about me from a hundred paces away.

As I entered his office and bowed I could see why I had been summoned. A letter bearing an all too familiar seal was being waved at me.

'I was beginning to wonder if we would ever see you again, Mercurius. Have you been in tavern company once more?'

'I have been to a tavern, yes, Rector, but I was solitary there.'

'Well, that's something I suppose,' he sniffed. 'This came for you today. It appears to be urgent, and the covering note tells me that I must expect you to be away for some time. The Stadhouder has graciously offered to cover your salary during your absence, with a little extra for the University for the inconvenience. If you will kindly give me a note of your teaching commitments before you leave, Mercurius, that would be appreciated.'

I gulped. I appeared to have no say in the matter.

'We may need your room so perhaps you would pack your personal items ready to go into store if necessary.'

I did not like the sound of that. It was almost as if the possibility of my resumption of my duties was being utterly discounted.

'As you direct, Rector,' I murmured.

'Stop looking so po-faced, man! I am only being practical. We look forward to your triumphant return in due course as usual. I am well aware that your efforts have redounded to the credit of this University, and that you have done much to ensure the Stadhouder's favour. We do not want to finish up like Nijmegen.'

No, we did not. The University of Nijmegen, founded to great acclaim in 1655, had recently been shuttered again and was not expected ever to reopen. It had been associated with unorthodox religious views and found its best staff tempted away by other universities. When the French invaded in 1672 and found a university teaching the theories of the detested René Descartes, which were thought to be highly uncatholic, they lost no time in closing the place down and scattering the staff. It tried to reopen in 1674, but finally gave up. It had become of so little account that nobody was quite sure when it had closed, but by 1682 every student and every lecturer had gone. Nobody in high places had championed its cause. The thought of it was bound to make any Rector shudder.

I accepted the letter with half-hearted thanks and made my way to my room with heavy tread, opening the door and staggering to the bed where I flopped down inelegantly. If only I had been as completely useless as an investigator as I thought I was. I never believed that I was any good at it, the only saving grace being that since nobody else was doing it at all the Stadhouder had no comparison to judge me against. Unfortunately I somehow kept succeeding despite my failings and imperfections, which I shall not list here. [No, Van der Meer, I will not, despite your coaxing. And no, you may not guess.]

If there was a silver lining to this particular cloud, it was that I recognised the handwriting of the letter as that of Bouwman, the Stadhouder's personal secretary. At times of urgency the Stadhouder was wont to write his own letters in his abominable scrawl. I have seen three-year-olds who formed their letters better. Be that as it may, the fact that Bouwman had written it indicated that there was no immediate panic. Against that, the willingness of the Stadhouder to reimburse the University for my salary suggested that this was a greater task than, for example, finding his lost slippers.

I pinched the corners of my eyes alongside my nose, sighed, and sat up to read this missive of doom. It began in the usual flowery way:

To our trusty and well-beloved servant, Master Mercurius, of the University of Leiden, greeting!

We find that we have need of your inestimable services once more. It would be appreciated if you would come to The Hague at your earliest convenience to attend to a matter of the greatest national importance.

His Excellency William of Orange,

Stadhouder.

Given this day at our palace at The Hague, the 28th day of February, 1685.

The dignified and composed nature of the epistle was marred to some degree by William's scrawled postscript.

Get your arse here now! Please. W.

I felt an overwhelming desire to bang my head against a wall until blessed unconsciousness supervened, but I resisted the temptation. Instead I dragged myself to the stairs and walked into the refectory to take my farewell of the blessed Mechtild, hoping that this angel of the kitchen would have some small consoling pastry for me.

Mechtild's husband, Albrecht, was the kitchen master, but allowed his wife to make bread and pastries and what are sometimes called dainties while he attended to the meats and, generally, anything that required a lot of flame. He enjoyed this so much that he extended the "lot of flame" to include a large number of things that did not normally need much cooking. I knew of no man in the entire University who was prepared to ask Albrecht to make him an omelette after we saw the blackened scraps he offered to one of the law lecturers.

His wife, on the other hand, was as delicate of touch as Albrecht was ham-fisted. Her gooseberry fool was so light that it was a wonder that it stayed in the bowl and did not head for the ceiling. Somehow her tartlets stayed golden despite being cooked in the same ovens that Albrecht had employed as a furnace for his roasts.

The mind-boggling part of this was that her hands appeared to be perfectly ordinary, if not rather pudgy. You expected the delicate fingers of a supreme embroiderer or tapestry-maker, and instead found the pink sausages of a rather tubby woman stuffed into a buff-coloured dress with her sleeves rolled up and a white apron that strained to keep everything inside when she lurched suddenly in some direction.

Mechtild looked up, and concern flitted over her features.

'You're going on one of your trips again, aren't you, Master?' she said.

'Yes, Mechtild. Does it show?'

'You've got a face like a wet sheep,' she replied. 'Come, sit down and we'll have a beaker of hot wine while you tell me about it.'

I obeyed meekly.

'I can't tell you much. I don't know why the Stadhouder wants me, but I wouldn't mind betting it has something to do with the King of England having just died.'

'God rest his soul,' mumbled Mechtild automatically. 'I'm prepared to swear that you were here when it happened.'

'I don't think I'm suspected of causing it, Mechtild. I just hope I don't have to go to England again. I hate sailing, it rains all the time there, and I can't understand some of the things they say. It's hard enough having to be polite and courtly, but being polite and courtly in English is exhausting.'

Mechtild produced a muslin cloth and unrolled it to reveal a little stack of almond biscuits. 'You look like you need one or two of these,' she smiled.

I don't know why I thought of her as a kindly aunt. She had no children that I knew of and she cannot have been much older than me, but there were times when I would gladly have laid my head on that ample bosom and accepted any comfort she offered, were it not for the fear that I might fall down the middle and suffocate. Instead, I allowed her to pat the back of my hand a couple of times.

'You finish your wine and biscuits and I'll see if I can't put a little bundle of something together for the journey,' she said.

If I ever get to be Pope, I thought, *I'll put you up for canonisation.*

That reminds me that I have not mentioned, as I always do, my little secret. Leiden is a bastion of the Reformed Church; that is, it is unswervingly Protestant. To lecture in the Faculty of Theology, as I do, one must be an ordained Protestant minister. Its existence is owed to the need for Protestant clergy.

I was ordained when my degree was completed, but I had already started to have some reservations about articles of doctrine. We need not go into detail here, but some Reformed teaching holds that only a certain number of us will get to Heaven, and God has already determined whom they should be. This seemed to me to remove hope from many of us; and if there is no hope of Paradise, why bother to live a good life? Why not drink and gamble and womanise and molest livestock? I do not know why I added that last example; I must have been mixing with men from Frisia again.

Anyway, in time I came to believe that the Catholic faith was to be preferred, and postgraduate study in France convinced me of this, so much so that I was ordained as a Catholic priest by the Bishop of Namur; however, the Bishop instructed me to keep my ordination secret because he was concerned that the Dutch might enforce the penal laws against Catholics and drive all the priests out of the country, if they did not burn them first. He wanted some priests to be available to rebuild the Dutch church if that happened. This suited me very well because it meant that I could keep my job at the University; after all, I was still an ordained Protestant minister. I had just been ordained again as something else.

This had been challenged by a case a few months earlier when a Catholic friar had been abducting Jewish children to have them brought up as Catholics, and I had discovered a number of prominent Catholics who did not see anything wrong with this, except that he had been caught. Accordingly, I was torn between the conviction that the doctrine of the Roman church was to be preferred with an increasing feeling that I did not belong there so long as that sort of thing was going on. It was all very uncomfortable.

I briefly reflected that when I last went to London a grateful King Charles had tried to give me the bishopric of Norwich, notwithstanding that I was not a member of the Church of England, something which he saw as a minor administrative matter easily rectified by Royal Command. In my present mood I was by no means sure that I would turn it down if it were offered again.

I accepted the parcel that Mechtild had prepared for me and, for the first time, found myself wrapped in her embrace. It was warm and tender, like being attacked by a mound of pillows.

'Go in peace, Master, and God grant you a safe return,' she whispered, and I noticed that she was crying a little.

For that matter, so was I.

CHAPTER TWO

Taking William at his word, I hired a horse for the journey to
The Hague. It was a bay gelding called Zeus, apparently
because he repeatedly issued thunderclaps from his rear end.
As I walked through the villages I found myself unnecessarily
explaining to passers-by that the eruptions were the fault of the
horse, since they seemed to be looking at me censoriously.

Nevertheless, Zeus was a willing beast and before too long I
arrived once more at the Binnenhof. The guards inspected my
travelling bag with care, unrolling the cloth containing
Mechtild's gift and eyeing the contents appreciatively.

'Got a new cook, have you?' asked the Sergeant, who always
referred to me as the Man with the Murderous Pie after an
occasion when I took one of Albrecht's pies with me and had
it confiscated on the grounds that you could kill someone by
hitting him with the crust. I did not object since it saved me
the trouble and pain of trying to bite into the thing.

'His wife,' I replied.

The Sergeant carefully rewrapped the parcel and returned it
to me. 'They're not a well matched couple, are they?' he said.

Conducted within, I was passed from guard to guard until I
finally found myself outside William's audience chamber.
Bouwman came to greet me.

'There will be a short delay, I'm afraid, Master Mercurius.
His Excellency is closeted with the new English ambassador,
Bevil Skelton.'

Bouwman winced as we heard William's raised voice. Clearly
the interview was not going well, a point demonstrated by the
twin evidences that we could hear what was being said, and

William was speaking Dutch rather than French or English. Skelton was replying in French and appeared equally heated.

'What are they arguing about?' I asked, then realised that I ought not to have done so, since it would require Bouwman to reveal his master's confidential business.

'Since I am not in the room I cannot be sure,' Bouwman replied, 'but I expect it has to do with the Duke of Monmouth. It usually does.'

'This is a repeated quarrel, then?'

Bouwman sighed. 'When will it end? You will know that King James has ascended to the throne and has demanded that the Spanish expel Monmouth from the Spanish Netherlands, where he has been living. Monmouth came here, to Rotterdam, and now the English want him expelled from there as well. Skelton tries to claim that they do not mean to hound him from country to country but that his presence so close to England is not conducive to the safety of the realm, as they quaintly put it.'

'And the Stadhouder won't expel him?'

'No, for three reasons. The Stadhouder actually likes him; they share an interest in soldiering and each respects the other's generalship. The Princess Mary has known Monmouth since she was a child and would hate any evil to befall him. And the Stadhouder resents being told what to do in his own country.'

I was not altogether sure that these three points were listed in the correct order of importance. There was no doubt in my mind that William would react badly to being given orders.

The door opened, and Skelton reversed out, pausing to bow politely in the doorway. I hoped that he did not speak Dutch, because William had just told him in the bluntest possible terms where he could stick his ultimatum, and was sufficiently roused to follow Skelton out of the room so he could abuse him some more from the top of the stairs. Only then did he turn and notice me. I had it in mind to go and find something else to do for a few minutes while William resumed his customary good humour, but I was trapped.

'Master! Come in here. We need to talk,' he announced.

'At your service,' I replied.

The air was thick with some pungent herbs. William's asthma must have been giving him some trouble, because he had a brazier with a brass dish on top filled with some foul-smelling plants, the fumes from which he claimed eased the tightness in his chest. The aroma cannot have improved the English ambassador's humour, since it was likely that his clothes would smell of this loathsome mixture for some time, an olfactory souvenir of his dispute.

'That man,' William snarled, 'that man is...'

Words seemed to fail him, and I could suggest nothing suitable.

'A Francophile!' Williams finally spat. 'He brown-noses his way around King Louis and has the gall to come here and demand that we send the late King Charles' own son away. He's doing France's bidding, there's no doubt of that, and I'll wager that King James will do the same. How can we live in amity in those circumstances?'

I judged it best not to make any comment, but simply to let him rant for a while until his humours were better balanced. It took rather longer than I had expected.

'It's a provocation, that's what it is. King James has sent him because he knows that Skelton will rile me. The man holds us in contempt, Mercurius, but he'll get no joy from me. I will not order the Duke of Monmouth to leave the country. Apart from anything else, I want him where I can keep an eye on him.'

He paused to swallow a large mouthful of wine and had to gulp it down because another point of contention had occurred to him.

'It's not as if I've ever plotted against my father-in-law, though God knows he deserves it. It's all Uncle Charles' fault for dying like that. We may have detested each other but we had an understanding. Neither of us would work against the other. We might argue about each other's bad points but we respected the good qualities we had. Charles was no fool, Mercurius, and he understood politics. Sometimes you have to say things you don't really mean. We had a code, Mercurius, did you know that? If he sent me a despatch I knew whether he really meant it or it was one of those things you have to say for the sake of appearances but you don't honestly mean.'

He motioned me to sit down and waved an arm extravagantly in the general direction of Amsterdam, which would have been fine had he not had half a goblet of wine in that hand at the time, which slopped against a hanging. Bouwman rushed to dab it with a cloth.

'You remember when I sent you to Amsterdam to spy on the English exiles there? Charles sent me a note saying that he wanted them sent back to face justice, but I knew from the code that what he really wanted was for us to keep them here and just tell him if they were planning an invasion. So long as it was just rebellious talk he was very happy to leave them in peace in our land, and so was I, because they spent plenty of money.'

I was beginning to wonder when William would tell me why he had summoned me to The Hague, but it sounded as if he had a deal more to get off his chest first.

'You're very quiet, Mercurius.'

'I didn't think any comment of mine would be helpful, Stadhouder.'

'I always value your views, man. You know that.'

'I'm not entirely clear why you wanted me here, Your Excellency,' I said hesitantly.

'Isn't it obvious?'

'Not to me, I'm afraid.'

William favoured me with one of his enigmatic half-smiles. 'No, well, you don't really understand politics, do you, Mercurius?'

'Not like you do, Stadhouder,' I flattered him.

It is true that I do not understand politics. I have no interest in such things, nor do I wish to inform myself because I cannot help noticing that a lot of people who show a keen interest in political matters end up on the scaffold.

'It's really very simple,' William began, dropping into a chair and inhaling deeply from the brazier. 'Who is the natural enemy of this country and the greatest threat to European peace?'

'King Louis of France,' I answered at once. Whether it was true or not, I cannot say, but I had heard the answer from William's own lips so many times that it required no thought.

'See! You do understand politics after all. If an unworldly man like you can see that — no offence, Master — I wonder why so many others can't? Anyway, it is a cardinal military maxim that you always face your greatest enemy first, so all other considerations are secondary when compared with the essential political aim of giving Louis a metaphorical kick in the ribs. In fact, I wouldn't rule out an actual kick in the ribs if the opportunity arose, but that's another matter. Now, Louis is untouchable at present, but his friends are not, and he has no greater friend than King James. Therefore, whatever James wants, he isn't going to get it from me until he gives up his friendship with Louis.'

'But if James is deposed doesn't that mean that your wife's claim to the throne evaporates?' I asked.

'Aha! Indeed it does, Mercurius. Well remarked! Perhaps I should think about appointing you to my council of state.'

I'd really rather you didn't, I thought, but I forced a reluctant smile.

'That's why I'm keeping James informed about Monmouth's plans, entirely out of the goodness of my heart, I'll have you know. I've half a mind to stop and if James asks why I'll blame that buffoon Skelton. He can't understand that if I kick Monmouth out I won't be able to tell James what he's doing. It's coming to something when I know what is in England's interests better than their ambassador does, Mercurius.'

'If you say so, Your Excellency.'

'I do say so, Mercurius, emphatically. But the point is that Monmouth is a good man, a friend. He keeps my wife happy with his company. I don't want any harm to befall him, Mercurius. He is being encouraged by a couple of reckless Scots who believe that he only has to show his face in England and the masses will flock to his banner in some kind of bloodless revolution. There's no such thing as a bloodless revolution, Mercurius, and the key question is whose blood is going to be spilt.'

Not mine, I hoped. I dislike the sight of blood at the best of times, and how I would react to seeing a puddle of my own was a regular concern of mine when working for the Stadhouder. William was the sort of man who, if his arm were lopped off during a battle, would take a sword in the other hand and dismiss his injury as naught but a scratch. I often whimper if I nick myself shaving. We were not cut from the same cloth.

'Forgive me, Your Excellency, but how can you keep a man from harm if he is set on a battle?'

'A very good question, Mercurius. I can see how right I was to send for a university man.'

To be brutally honest, even one of my undergraduates could have come up with that objection. You did not need a degree and twenty years of teaching experience to work out that battles are dangerous and people get hurt during them. I once picked up a pike and got a very nasty splinter in the palm of my hand that was a devil to get out.

'The trick is to convince him that he can't win, but that he can withdraw with honour to prevent the futile shedding of blood, principally his own. If James acts on our advice, he'll assemble a large army exactly where it is needed and block Monmouth's way to London. Monmouth is brave and has a high sense of honour, but he's not foolhardy. If he sees there's no way past, he'll retire and try again some other day.'

'And will King James listen to advice?'

'He never has before,' admitted William. 'And now this idiot Skelton has persuaded him to discount my intelligence because I want to manoeuvre the English army out of the way so that Monmouth can capture the capital. Or even invade myself! Why invade, Mercurius, when I come into the kingdom without effort as soon as James is dead?' William summoned me to look at a map on his desk. 'This is England. That's London there. Monmouth's plan is to start risings in various places and have armies converge on London from all sides, recruiting as they go. His own entry will be in the south-west, somewhere near Exeter, where he has high hopes of support, the local populace being disaffected.'

'Isn't that a long way from London?'

'About ten days' march, I believe, and that's a serious drawback to his plan. On the other hand, it probably gives him a week to recruit troops and build a large army before James engages him. I told James all this and suggested that he move his army partway to Exeter; somewhere like Salisbury. There's a large plain there where an army can be camped and arrayed without difficulty, but Skelton has persuaded him that if he does that Monmouth and I will quickly sail up the Thames and snatch London before he can turn his army around. I have to convince James that I'm being scrupulously honest, but he'll not hear it.'

'A pretty problem indeed,' I agreed. 'There are none so blind as those who will not see.'

'Exactly, Mercurius. But then I had a brainwave.'

My stomach contracted violently at his words. I knew where his brainwaves led.

'King James is a Catholic. He surrounds himself with Catholics. He trusts Catholics. If you were a Catholic he would trust you.'

If only you knew, I thought, but held my peace.

'He is suspicious of Protestants. We Dutch are staunch Protestants, therefore he distrusts us. Monmouth is a Protestant, so he distrusts him too. He will always assume that we Dutch are supporting Monmouth, even if it appears not to be in our interests, because Protestants always stick together.'

'But if it is obviously not in our interests, Stadhouder, surely he will revise his opinion?'

'James is an anointed King, Mercurius, but holy oil doesn't make your brain work better. My horse is a deeper thinker than my father-in-law.'

It was true that James was reputed not to be at the forefront of European intellectual life, but few kings were; and I had met him. He might not be outstandingly intelligent but he was not a complete fool. He was dogmatic and rather blinkered, and I could well imagine him thinking just as William had outlined, but I would not esteem his wits so poorly.

'So what do you propose to do, Your Excellency?'

William smiled broadly. 'It's not about what I'm going to do, Mercurius. It's about what *you're* going to do.'

'Me?' I squeaked. I repeated the ejaculation in a lower, more manly register and tried to pretend I had a cough.

'Yes, you, Mercurius. You're a Protestant minister. He will naturally mistrust you. In James' mind, you will be unequivocally for Monmouth. Of course you'll deny it, and you'll be utterly sincere in that, but it will make no difference. James will be even more convinced that he is right when you deny it.'

'I'm going to London, am I?' I stammered weakly.

'Yes! I'm sending you to confer with the Bishop of London. I believe you know each other?'

'Mijnheer Compton?'

'That's the fellow. Ostensibly you'll be conferring about bringing the Church of England and the Dutch Reformed Church closer together. Our Ambassador over there has arranged the whole thing. You'll have a couple of pleasant dinners together, then he'll send you to see the Bishop of Exeter for a second opinion. While you're there I want you to ask a few questions about the city's defences — nothing too detailed, you understand, just the kind of thing that a clergyman wouldn't normally trouble himself about. Then — and this is the important bit — you lose the envelope I'm going to give you.'

'Lose an envelope?'

'Not just any envelope, Mercurius. An envelope containing Monmouth's highly confidential invasion plans. You have to lose it somewhere it's certain to be found after you've gone. Then it will be passed to King James, and because it came from you and it'll look like you inadvertently left it behind, he'll believe what it says. He'll move his armies, Monmouth will be scared off, and we'll all live happily ever after.'

I could see a potential flaw in this plan. 'Won't the English arrest me as a spy and hang me?'

William tutted. 'It's very unlikely,' he said. 'Possible, I suppose, but very unlikely. Hang a clergyman? Think of the international reaction. A lot of European powers would be rather upset.'

As would I, only I'd be the one who was upset with his neck in a noose. 'And how will I escape, Your Excellency?'

'That's the beauty of the plan, Mercurius. The ship that takes you to England will also take you from London to Exeter and then wait there to bring you back home. It's a lovely little thing. I picked it myself. Very fast and manoeuvrable.'

'What if the winds are contrary, Stadhouder?'

'Are you determined to pick holes in this plan, Mercurius? If you can't get straight back to Hellevoetsluis the master will take you somewhere safe. Not France, obviously. Maybe Ireland.'

'Isn't Ireland a notoriously Catholic country?' I asked.

'That's a point,' conceded William.

I began to have my doubts about how well-conceived this plan was.

William inspected the map. 'Perhaps Portugal,' he said. 'No, that's Catholic too. Maybe this place here. What's that?'

'Iceland, Stadhouder.'

'That'll do. They'll never look for you there. A few weeks lying low, then you can sail back across the top of Scotland. Well, what do you say, Mercurius?'

It will come as no surprise to the alert reader that having asked the question William promptly strode from the room before I could answer. The possible responses that I was turning over in my mind were all quite negative, including one which, if my grandmother had heard it, would have earned me a cuff round the ear for vulgarity. I can only plead that the stress of my position overpowered my better judgement; but it was all to no avail, because William had taken it for granted that I would assent. I just stood there dumbfounded and speechless.

William poked his head back around the door. 'Aren't you coming for supper?' he said. 'My wife's keen to meet you again.'

CHAPTER THREE

When you read accounts of executions they quite often include the phrase "The condemned man ate a hearty breakfast". I think the writers put that in just to make the rest of us feel better, because I cannot imagine anyone having much of an appetite knowing that in a couple of hours he will be slowly strangled or lying in pieces on a scaffold.

My appetite had certainly diminished once I had been told that I was going to England once again. It was not just that England was a godless and insanitary disgrace to the planet, though it undoubtedly was, or at least London was; it was the thought of being asked to undertake a task to which I was temperamentally unsuited. What line of thought would make a ruler think "I need someone to undertake a perilous cloak and dagger mission in a strange land. I know, I'll ask a university lecturer"?

My past adventures had demonstrated that I have an uncanny knack for putting myself in peril. At least four times I had been subjected to a murderous attack, on three occasions when I was working for our beloved Stadhouder, and once when on an enquiry of my own, and I could not help but think that one day my luck might run out.

I am not a hero. I do not have the reflexes of one. There are men, I understand, who react to danger to others by selflessly interposing themselves. They are to be admired, but not emulated, at least not by a middle-aged philosophy lecturer. Faced with an assassin with a knife my natural reaction is to get behind someone else, not in front of them; and while it is not easy to run fast in a clerical gown I would be prepared to give it my best effort. The bravest thing I have ever done in my life is to eat Albrecht's cooking.

I was invited to sit at Princess Mary's right hand, which was very pleasant. She was not conventionally beautiful, being a little too tall and somewhat ungainly, though she was an enthusiastic dancer. Her husband was not, and tended to approach dancing rather like a military exercise, attempting to outflank his partner by sudden unpredictable movements, but she was the one person who could entice him to trip a measure or two. Since she was half a head taller than him he preferred dances where the couples stood apart.

She was still a very young woman, in her early twenties at that time, but very mature in many ways. William trusted her judgement sufficiently to leave her to run the country in his absence, and she never let him down. She had great common sense and a keen intelligence, although to see anything that she had written you might not think so. She found spelling a challenge in both English and Dutch, but then that only puts her on a par with many of my students. The only superiority they show is that many also can't spell in Latin.

'Master Mercurius, it is so good to see you again,' she said.

'And I am delighted to see you too, Your Highness.'

'What brings you to The Hague, or can't you say?'

'His Excellency has a little job for me.'

'Oh, dear. I hope it won't be too tiresome.'

Tiresome? Probably not. Dangerous and foolhardy were the adjectives that came to mind, but I said nothing.

William was not one for fripperies and that extended to his food too. French sauces were definitely not encouraged, so our supper was relatively plain, though with some excellent fish and a large piece of roast beef that William sampled regularly during the evening.

'His Excellency is in a good humour,' I remarked.

'He always is when he is busy,' Princess Mary replied. 'He detests idleness.'

'Is there some particular cause for his activity?'

'Why, yes! My cousin's invasion plans.'

'They are real, then, madame?'

'Oh, certainly. I wonder that my father the King is not more exercised about them. You have met the new British Ambassador, I believe.'

'We passed in a corridor. I would not say that I have met him.'

'Lucky you. He is an odious man. Of course, he is unfailingly polite to me, since I may one day be his monarch and I might have a long memory, but he is horribly objectionable to poor Willy.'

I had never thought of the Stadhouder as a Willy. Indeed, the very idea that he might have a pet name had never crossed my mind. For that matter, I suppose he must have been a child once, though when I tried to picture it I saw a slightly smaller version of the William opposite me, still with a breastplate and a pistol in his sash.

'Forgive me, but I understood that the Stadhouder was not involving himself in the Duke of Monmouth's invasion plans.'

Mary carefully buttered a slice of bread before replying. 'He isn't. But that fool Skelton has completely missed the point. Not only does he refuse to believe that Monmouth will land in the south-west, but he thinks that all the plans are afoot in Rotterdam, where Monmouth is living, and since he sees no warships there he is quite relaxed. In fact, the warships are being made ready at Texel, to the north of Amsterdam. Monmouth is cunningly keeping well away so as not to draw attention to them.'

William had not mentioned this. 'Does that mean that the invasion is imminent?'

'Now, Master, how would a mere woman know such a thing?' said the Princess, dabbing her lips daintily with a napkin.

I knew her well enough to know that this description of herself as a mere woman was all pretence. There might be women whose whole world was bound up with fashion and tea-parties, but Mary was not one of them.

'It may be, for aught I know, that the poor Duke is compelled to sell all his household furnishings to meet the cost of the expedition, and that is sure to take some time. Then, of course, he must find another household for his wife and dispose of any mistresses that he might have. But there, I must not dispense gossip! All these things we silly women hear are completely unproven, after all.'

'But that he will lead a rebellion is certain?' I asked anxiously.

'Far from it!' said Mary. 'I know his mind better than most. He is naturally the most loyal of men, and it would go hard with him to oppose an anointed king; but he is being moved by his friends and acquaintances who tell him daily of the encumbrances of life in England now that my father is king.'

'Surely, madame, you know your father better than anyone here. Is he likely to make life in England so unpleasant that rebellion is necessary?'

Mary considered a moment. 'He is not a bad man, Master, but he has bad friends. He sees it as his mission to overturn a hundred and fifty years of history and restore England to the Catholic Church, but he knows it cannot be done by fiat. However, he believes — and may be right — that the mass of men in the country are sympathetic to the old ways and it is only a small elite group that is passionately committed to

Protestantism. Remove them, and the matter may be done. That primarily means the Whigs in parliament, and some of the bishops.'

'Only some of the bishops? Surely all the bishops of the Church of England hold to Protestantism?'

Mary looked surprised. 'Dear me, no! The bishops have never agreed on that or anything else and probably never will. That is one of the glories of the Church of England; it is so keen to be a national church encompassing as many people as possible that it tries very hard not to have any definite opinions on anything unless it positively must.' She took a sip from her wine goblet. 'I think it likely that most of them will agree that there are Ten Commandments and twelve apostles, but as for the rest…'

I am very fond of my bed. I suppose most people prefer to sleep in their own bed, and I have found very few others as comfortable over the years, but the bed provided for me at The Hague was magnificent. I had seen King Charles' bed at Whitehall, and even with Charles and the Duchess of Portsmouth on it there would have been plenty of room for a couple of others. My bed that night was not much its inferior in any respect, and I had it all to myself.

That made it all the more galling when I was woken at half past five in the morning by a servant with a jug of hot water and a dish of tea. Having tasted it I think I would rather have drunk the hot water and shaved with the tea, but I completed my toilet and presented myself in the great chamber as quickly as I could. William was stomping around ordering people in all directions while simultaneously reading from a sheaf of documents he clutched in one hand, Bouwman trailing behind him like a puppy trying to please his master.

'Mercurius! Good morning to you,' William bellowed. 'I'm sorry that we had to rouse you so early but no doubt you were up betimes for your morning prayers.'

It is the custom of some to begin their day with prayers at 6 a.m. and when I attend clerical conferences I have to steel myself to leave my warm bed and go to a cold church before breakfast. Working on the principle that prostration is a type of worship that shows the utmost respect to our Creator, I prefer to say my morning prayers prostrate in my bed, having rolled over onto my front.

'Is there some urgency then, Your Excellency?'

'You have a busy day ahead of you. I understand you are travelling light. That won't do for England, Mercurius. You'll need something to wear while the other outfits are drying out after the rain. Bouwman has found you a travelling chest and first thing this morning he'll take you to get some extra shirts and drawers. Then you set out for Hellevoetsluis to board your ship. It's thirty miles and you need to arrive before dark. You sail on the evening tide.'

I tried to look enthusiastic but failed dismally.

'I'll come with you to see you off. We can go in my carriage,' William proposed. He slapped me playfully on the back, which caused my teeth to judder a little. 'And I'll hand you the letter at the very last minute,' he said in a stage whisper which he probably intended to be a real whisper. William wasn't too good at keeping his voice down. 'It wouldn't do for you to lose it, would it?' he chuckled.

I nibbled on some bread and silently mused on the desirability of making my will before I left. The chief argument against that was the realisation that I did not have anyone to leave anything to; a secondary consideration was that I did not have much to leave. There were my books, which the library at the University would probably want to have, and there was my secret deposit of gold at the goldsmith's. Someone going through my papers after my passing might find the receipt. It occurred to me that I should really have made some arrangement before leaving Leiden because now I would have no say in the destination of my gold, and I resolved to attend to the matter as soon as might be following my return. [Yes, Van der Meer, I did, and no, I'm not telling you what will happen to it when I die. You'll have to wait and see. By the way, you'll find you can't write with crossed fingers.]

As a minister of the church I do not spend a lot of time clothes shopping, because our garments are more or less dictated for us. However, spare shirts and underthings never come amiss, so I meekly followed Bouwman as he led me to various merchants who were prepared to extend credit to the Stadhouder. I can only hope they were paid in due course, because I should hate to have my underclothes repossessed; and, frankly, if you supplied the drawers I was wearing towards the end of this tale you probably wouldn't want them back.

Around half past ten we returned to the Binnenhof and I had a few moments to say my farewells to Bouwman and Princess Mary before our departure. The princess was charming, assuring me of her prayers for my safe return and offering me her hand to kiss. As I grasped it she gave my fingers a gentle squeeze. She made me feel as if I were about to slay a dragon on her behalf.

Descending to the courtyard I found my borrowed chest being lashed to the carriage while William inspected the accompanying troop of horse. When he was satisfied we boarded his carriage and set out for Hellevoetsluis.

Hellevoetsluis is an odd place. You will find it in the south of the country a little to the south-west of Rotterdam, on a small tongue of land that has water on either side. Originally this was a muddy delta of various waterways, full of silt and largely disregarded, until someone had the idea of gouging docks into the mud and building a large harbour. The beauty of the site is that it opens onto a wide river rather than the sea and is therefore unlikely to be found by any foe by chance. Moreover, due to some clever engineering it is heavily fortified. Any enemies trying to attack it would have to run the gauntlet of cannon on both sides and would need to proceed in a narrow file along a canal into a walled city. These advantages have made Hellevoetsluis the base for our navy, and since almost everyone who lives there relies directly or indirectly on the navy for their livelihood they are remarkably close-mouthed about what goes on there. William explained to me as we trotted along the road to Rotterdam that every time Skelton went there his every move, each question that he asked and the names of those to whom he spoke were reported to him before Skelton was back at The Hague. At William's instigation the local officials had spun Skelton a yarn about a certain mijnheer Stommerd who had, allegedly, hired a couple of gunships to protect his ships bound for Suriname. If Skelton had spoken Dutch he might have been surprised to hear that anyone bore the surname Dimwit; it tickled William to think of the response Skelton would have received to his despatches to London recording the hire when they were read by any of the King's advisers who spoke Dutch.

William was not one to waste travelling time on food and drink. He ate sparingly and apart from a stop so that he could make water in a hedge, an activity interrupted by an irate farmer's wife, much to William's amusement, we kept travelling until we arrived at Hellevoetsluis and I first had the opportunity to cast my eye over the *Nieuwpoort*.

I am no judge of a sailing vessel, but even I could see that this was built for speed. It sat high in the water as if merely skimming the surface, and it carried a lot of sail for a relatively small boat.

'Beautiful, isn't she?' asked William with some pride in his voice. 'She's built narrow in the beam so she cuts through the water like an arrow. Of course, she's less stable than some in a storm, so the master will heave close to land if the weather turns nasty, and I doubt she'll see much sailing in a bad winter. But for a quick springtime dash across to London, she is just the thing. I almost wish I were going with you.'

Why don't you? I thought. *Then you could lose your own letter.* Naturally I said nothing of the sort, but complimented him on his ship's elegance.

'She looks as stately as the Princess,' I said, at which William looked at me oddly, then broke into a wide grin.

'Do you know, I couldn't have put it better myself! There's quite a resemblance, isn't there.'

He continued pleased with my comment for some time, repeating it to several naval officers he met and to the landlord of an inn where I took my last supper.

'No appetite, Mercurius?' William called down the table.

'I'm not a good sailor, Your Excellency,' I replied.

'Does anyone have any advice for my dear friend Mercurius?' William asked our companions.

A young naval officer spoke up. 'I heartily recommend drinking your fill of good port wine and passing the entire journey sleeping it off in your bunk. At least that's what I always do!'

There was uproarious laughter on all sides. I forced a faint smile.

'You haven't met Captain Velders, have you?' William asked. 'It's good that you've taken to each other — he's commanding your ship.'

In the light of this new information I prayed sincerely that he was joking when he made his remark.

'At your service, Master,' said Velders with an exaggerated courtly bow.

William walked round the table and crouched beside me. 'He's good at his job, the best you could have for this mission,' he said. 'You'll be in safe hands with Velders. You can trust him with anything. He knows your mission and he will obey your commands without question and bring you home safely. Now, the top letter is the one you need to lose. The one beneath is a letter accrediting you as a diplomat of my court. It's probably best if you don't muddle them up. If you get into trouble you may use it to get yourself out of a scrape, but only use it if absolutely necessary. If the English know you've come on my behalf they'll treat you with suspicion and you won't be able to accomplish your mission.'

I wanted to ask why I needed such a letter if the mission I had been set was as safe and straightforward as William had insisted it would be. Under what circumstances might I find myself in prison, I wondered?

There was no time to ask, because William plucked me from my chair and frogmarched me to the ship.

'Time to go. God speed, Mercurius.' He clapped me on the arm. 'I won't forget this,' he said.

I won't either, I thought. *Let's hope it is unforgettable for the right reasons.*

CHAPTER FOUR

If sailing on the open sea struck me as hazardous, sailing in the dark seemed to me to be foolhardy in the extreme. Unfortunately, as Captain Velders patiently explained, it is not always possible to put into port at sunset, and the ship carried lights, though these never seemed bright enough to me. Besides, Velders added, there would always be someone watching out for other ships with whom we might collide.

'What are you worried about?' Velders asked.

'I don't know. Whales? Pirates?'

'There aren't many whales here and the only successful pirates in the North Sea are us,' he chuckled. 'You may sleep soundly, Master. No ill will befall you here.'

Sleep? Who can sleep on a ship? I suppose sailors have to learn to do so, since they cannot stay awake for months on end; but as to what sort of person would choose the sea as a career, I do not choose to think. A ship is like a floating dungeon, and on top of that you have to worry about what will happen if it stops floating.

My late brother Laurentius joined the navy and loved the nautical life, which he described as being filled with adventure and new sights. I've lived in Leiden for thirty years, and there are still sights there I haven't seen, so that will do me nicely. I have no wish to visit the Indies or see China.

After all, my foreign trips had not been encouraging. I disliked France, and I did not care if I never set foot in England again; though come to think of it, I did care if that meant I had to stay on board this glorified raft. Drowning did not appeal to me either. If the ship sank perhaps nobody would ever find out what had happened to us.

In this cheerful frame of mind I took myself off to my cabin at the back of the ship — please, reader, do not expect nautical terminology from me — and decided to read the letter that I was supposed to leave behind me. It seemed to me that it had to have been visibly opened and read if it were to convince anyone that it was genuine.

Unfortunately I had been presented with two letters, and when I opened my travelling chest they appeared to have moved with the rocking of the ship. I held them up to the light and confidently selected the one that contained the rebellion plans.

Here is a small tip that you may find useful someday. If you warm a fine blade, you can slide it under the wax of a seal and lift the seal unbroken. Just in case I was wrong, that was what I decided to do, which was just as well, because it turned out that I had the missives confused, and the one I had opened was the letter accrediting me as a diplomat, so I hurriedly resealed it, warming the underside of the wax with my blade and pressing it firmly back down. I will not claim that it was a flawless resealing but it would pass reasonable inspection and the Stadhouder's seal was intact.

I then turned my attention to the second envelope and did the same thing. It consisted of a large sheet of paper with an enclosed map. The map was easy enough to identify, particularly since London and a few other cities were marked on it, with major roads shown in red ink and the movement of armies indicated by arrows. The accompanying sheet gave details of the manoeuvre, allegedly addressed to the Earl of Shaftesbury, though whether he knew anything of the matter was not clear. At any event, when this was found he would be assumed to be one of the rebels, so I hoped that it was true and that he was prepared for it. Knowing William, the thought of warning Shaftesbury had probably never crossed his mind.

I had to admit it was a good forgery. If I had not known it to be the work of someone in William's pay I would have been convinced. I carefully folded the papers exactly as they had been and reassembled the package. Clearly the papers were more likely to be believed if they had been read, for which purpose they must be opened, but since the enclosure was important I decided to reseal the letter to prevent the map falling out. Once again I warmed my penknife over a candle, softened the underside of the seal, and pressed it back into place.

It was then that I spotted the terrible error that threatened to undermine the whole plot. The letters were identical because William had sealed both with his own seal. Surely if anyone found this letter and believed the contents they would naturally assume that this meant that William was part of the plotters, although he had sworn on his honour that he was not. Somehow I had to replace the seal with another seal, but I had nothing to do it with. The only thing I could think of was to carefully amend the Stadhouder's seal until it was unrecognisable, but that would have to wait until morning, when the light was better. I tucked the two letters inside my chest, one at the front and the other at the back, fastened the lid once more and lay down to try to get some sleep.

At some horribly antisocial hour someone knocked loudly at my door to announce that breakfast was ready. I hurriedly splashed my face with some water, donned my gown and followed the sailor to the small room where breakfast was being served.

When I had boarded the ship all was activity and I had gone first to my cabin to stow my belongings and keep out of the way in case they gave me a job to do. I am not unwilling, but I can never quite work out which rope to pull to achieve the desired end, nor can I remember the stupid names they give the sails. Why they cannot simply call them front, middle and back, or one, two and three is beyond me. People claim that sailors are dullards, but it must be hard to interpret a command to reef the mizzen staysail, or whatever they say, rather than asking "Would one of you roll up the sail at the pointy end?"

I took my place at the officers' table where Captain Velders introduced me to Lieutenant Hendriks, his second-in-command. Hendriks must just have come off watch, because he was wearing a thick oilcloth cloak and his cheeks were reddened.

'We're making good speed,' announced Velders. 'At times we've been making eight knots. If all is well, we should make England tomorrow morning.'

'God be praised,' I said. I intended only to think it, but somehow the words came out. I do that sometimes.

'I perceive that you are not a practised sailor, Master,' Hendriks commented.

'Almost a novice,' I replied. 'I sailed to London eight years ago, but in a rather larger vessel.'

'Larger, and therefore slower!' Velders said. 'Take comfort, Master, that there is no quicker way of crossing the sea than this. We are about one-third of the way there now.'

That still leaves two-thirds of this misery to come, I thought, *not to mention the return journey*.

'Are the winds kind to us?' I asked.

'They are not perfect, being slightly from the north-east, but they will suffice,' Hendriks remarked. 'They're strong enough and not contrary, and that's good enough for us.'

'Confidentially, Master,' Velders added, 'Hendriks here is the sailor among us. I have learned enough, but he has been sailing since he was a boy. I just point the ship in the right direction and keep going. Hendriks can coax the very best from any wind he is given.'

I am no sailor, but I am sure that there is more to oceanic navigation than pointing the ship in the right direction and keeping going. For one thing, I have seen the route to the East Indies on a globe, and it seems to me to require several turns, particularly as you pass South Africa, when there is a sharp left turn that must be made if you are not to run aground on the snowy wastes of Antarctica. Not that I was averse to running aground in the right circumstances; better that than missing England altogether and continuing out into the Atlantic Ocean.

I was brought a hot drink which, I understand, is made from brandy mixed with hot water. It helps to keep the cold out and sailors are very fond of it. Since it was a short voyage, the food was still fresh, so I enjoyed some bread and bacon.

'How do you cook on a ship?' I asked.

'Bless you, Master,' said the sailor serving us, 'we have an oven below decks.'

'An oven? With a fire? Inside a wooden ship?'

My agitation must have conveyed itself forcibly because Velders laughed as he replied. 'My dear Master, rest easy! The oven is encased in bricks for that very reason; and one of the good things about a fire at sea is that you are never short of water to put it out.'

Velders excused himself to go to receive the report of the young officer currently in charge of the ship, so I sat a little longer with Hendriks until he said that he must stow his wet clothes and then grab some sleep before his next watch. The sailor brought me another cup of hot brandy and water which I sipped contentedly until my eye was caught by a small stand on the chart desk at the back of the room.

The stand contained various seals that might be used. Inspecting each in turn, I found one that I did not recognise. There was nobody to ask, and I only needed it for a few moments, so I tucked it in my sleeve to use to replace William's seal on the letter that I was instructed to lose.

I climbed to the deck where Velders was deep in discussion with a very young officer, so I decided not to interrupt, but to return at once to my cabin to undertake my task. I sat on my little bed and opened the shutters as far as I could to allow me the maximum light. My candle had gone out and I went in search of one to light it from, finding one in a lamp in the galley. I was now ready to begin my career as a master forger.

I knelt by my chest, and immediately something caught my eye. There was something strange about the knot.

I must explain that the chest was fastened using a thin rope. The rope passed through two holes in the lid, and two holes in the base. The loose ends were then knotted. This prevented the chest coming undone in transit, but was not particularly secure. Ideally, we would have had a chain rather than a rope.

I had closed it the previous night, and it was still closed, but there was something different about the knot. I was as sure as I could be that I had knotted it with the only kind of knot I know, but now the knot appeared more complex. Instead of a bow, it now had a slip knot.

I hurried to unfasten it and inspect the contents of my chest. Flinging the lid back I plunged my hand inside and felt for the letters. There was one at the front, but none at the back.

Panicking, I emptied the whole contents of the chest on the bed. I unfolded clothes, shook books and examined boots but the second letter was not there. I had lost the rebellion letter, or, more accurately, it had been stolen.

I rushed to find Velders, first tucking the other letter inside my shirt for safe keeping. I had lost one; I did not mean to lose both.

'The letter!' I said. 'It's gone!'

Velders grabbed me by the arm and hurried me below decks. 'Let us not discuss this matter in the hearing of others,' he said. 'Now, what do you mean, it's gone?'

I am not deficient in literacy, but I could not think of any appropriate synonyms that might make my meaning clearer. 'It's gone. Vanished. Disappeared. It's not there.'

Velders did not appear too concerned. 'Well, you were told to lose it, and you've lost it. What's the problem?'

'I have to lose it in the right place, and this is not the right place.'

'Calm yourself, Master. We're on board a ship. There are not many places it can go.'

'It could have been thrown overboard. We must turn round and look for it.'

Velders emitted a deep sigh. 'Master, a ship is not like a horse. It leaves no tracks. And the sea is vast. The chances that anything lost overboard can be found are negligible.'

'But we must try!'

'Master, when did you last see the letter?'

'Last night, just before I went to sleep. I put it in my chest and secured it.'

'That's ten hours or more ago. We've travelled over seventy miles since then, Master. If we find it it'll be soaked through and unusable.'

I had to admit that Velders had a point. If it had been thrown overboard it was lost. 'But it may still be on the boat somewhere.'

'The ship. Yes, it could be on the ship. We'll organise a search.'

He ordered a nearby seaman to find Hendriks who appeared within a few minutes, bleary-eyed from his disturbed sleep. Apprised of the disaster which had befallen me, he suggested a division of the ship such that he searched the port side and Velders would take the starboard side; or perhaps it was the other way round. And perhaps it was Velders who suggested it. I do not really know. I was rather overwrought at this point.

The two officers began their search while I completed a detailed examination of my cabin. All the men's kitbags were opened and examined, and the whole ship from top to bottom was searched, but after a couple of hours they came to me to announce that they had had no luck. The letter was not to be found anywhere.

Meanwhile, I had been thinking. In order to want to steal the letter, you must know of its existence; and the only person I knew for sure knew that it existed was Captain Velders. But what possible motive could he have for its theft? And, given that it was not on the ship, why would he destroy it having stolen it? Who gained from its destruction?

A little thought suggested that King James could not benefit, because it was in his interest to know what Monmouth was planning so that he could prepare for it. Monmouth, then? I supposed that anything that gave Monmouth any advantage, even the relatively small one of maintaining some surprise, was worth pursuing, but that depended on whether Velders knew what was in the letter. What exactly had William told him when he briefed him?

'We'll have to turn round,' I said. 'There's no point in going any further if I don't have a letter to lose, is there?'

'But you have meetings arranged, Master. How will it look if you don't turn up?' Velders replied.

He had a point. Apart from anything else, it would impinge on my personal trustworthiness, because nobody would know why I had done that. On the other hand, how could I complete a mission without the tools I had been given? It was like sending an army out with muskets but no ammunition.

'And how am I to obey the Stadhouder's instructions without the documents I was supposed to deliver?' I asked.

'Surely you're not meant to deliver them anyway?' answered Velders. 'The point was to lose them, and you've lost them.'

There was no solution other than to ask him outright what he knew.

'Did the Stadhouder tell you what was in the envelope?'

'Yes. He said they were secret plans of the Duke of Monmouth's that must be delivered to King James and that you had instructions on how to do so.'

That disposed of any idea that Velders had taken them believing them to be something else. If he had taken them, he knew what he was doing. Despite William's trust in him, that could only mean that Velders was working for the Duke of Monmouth, preventing his plans from being disclosed to his enemy.

Of course, it might not have been Velders at all. Suppose William's plan had become common knowledge around Hellevoetsluis? Any of the sailors might have been seduced with money to steal the letter. At any event, whoever did it, they had apparently disposed of the evidence and the crime could never be brought home to them.

I felt dejected and defeated. 'I'm going back to my cabin. Leave me alone until we arrive in London,' I muttered, and trudged back through the ship, entered my room and bolted the door behind me. I sighed a few times, slipped off my boots and lay down on the bed.

The chest was as I had left it this time, and I remembered that I still had the other letter in my shirt which I could put in the chest now that I did not intend to leave the room, so I unfastened the rope once again, reached inside my shirt, and made to put the letter in the chest.

Just a minute, I told myself.

This letter was the thicker of the two. It felt as if a smaller sheet had been folded inside a larger one. Hurriedly I lit a candle and warmed my penknife once more, sliding it in a rather ham-fisted way under the seal to prise the letter open.

It was the Duke's plans. The letter that had been stolen was actually my letter of accreditation as a diplomat. Who would want that, since it clearly bore my name inside?

It was all a bit much for my brain at that moment, but as I dozed the answer came to me. There might be people who knew of the important letter but they did not know — any more than I had done before William told me at Hellevoetsluis — that there was a second letter. When the culprit rifled my chest he stopped when he found a letter. He didn't go on looking until he found the second one. Believing that he had retrieved what he was sent for, he had thrown it overboard and considered his mission accomplished.

If he found out that I still had the letter he must surely try again to steal it; but if I did not disclose my new knowledge the letter would be safe.

My only course of action was plain. I must go round with a hangdog expression looking like I had lost the letter and failed in my mission. Nobody must know that the thief had stolen the wrong letter.

On the other hand, I had been looking forward to claiming diplomatic privileges. I didn't know what they were, but there must be some advantages to being an ambassador, or nobody would want the job, especially if it meant that they had to live in London.

CHAPTER FIVE

In the privacy of my cabin, I slowly held the wax seal over the candle until the surface was softened. Using the flat blade of my penknife, I gently smoothed the surface of the wax to obliterate any evidence that William had sealed the document. By this time the wax was setting once more, and I had to hold it over the flame again to melt the surface for striking a new seal.

The seal I had borrowed was around the same size and bore heraldic arms, so that was good enough for me. I had no idea whose it might be but it did not really matter, because I planned to use it so inexpertly that the impression would be unclear anyway. A little bit of smudging never hurt anyone.

I am delighted to say that doing things inexpertly comes naturally to me, and I was very pleased with the result. The letter had plainly been sealed by some gentleman of status, and one who had an animal of some kind on his arms though whether it was a lion, a horse or even a unicorn was hard to tell. It might have been a lion rampant, but it might equally have been an old woman waving.

Now all that remained for me to do was to return the seal to the room from which I had taken it, and my work would be complete. I tucked the letter inside my shirt once more and made my way to the room. Inconveniently, Lieutenant Hendriks was sitting there when I entered so I had to invent some reason to have gone there.

'You won't mind if I finish eating?' Hendriks asked politely.

'By no means. Please continue.'

'I could send for a dish of beans for you if you wish to join me?'

'Thank you. I'm not sure I could eat just at the moment. Or indeed before we reach dry land.'

'If I may, Master, it's easier to throw up on a full stomach than an empty one.'

I was unconvinced; and to be honest I had no plans to throw up on any kind of stomach. I have a strong preference for food that has gone down to stay down. Just looking at Hendriks' plate was making me feel rather queasy. I turned away instinctively and found myself leaning on the chart table for support.

'Are you quite well, Master?' Hendriks asked solicitously.

'Not all that wonderful just at the moment,' I admitted, clapping a hand over my mouth to suppress any rising bile. Sad to relate, the sudden upward movement of my arm caused the seal hidden in my sleeve to drop to the floor with a loud click. I moved to pick it up but Hendriks was already stooping.

'I'll get it…' he began but was cut off by the need to massage his temple as we banged heads in a very inelegant way.

'I'm sorry, I'm so clumsy,' I murmured.

'Not to worry, Master. There's no harm done. The captain's seal must have fallen off the bench.'

He returned it to the rack.

This might be slightly awkward, I thought. I have now implicated the captain in the Monmouth conspiracy, which could make life very difficult for me if he happened to be innocent. On the other hand, he was the prime suspect in the theft of my letter, so he deserved everything he got.

I had to take myself in hand and regain a sense of proportion about this. Stealing a letter that I'd only had in my possession for a few hours might be highly aggravating but it was not a major crime. Being a member of a conspiracy to overthrow a foreign government would probably have graver consequences. I thought the seal was sufficiently smudged not to be definitely attributable to anyone, but suppose I was wrong? Maybe I owed it to Velders to rework the seal once more, but if so, how? My skills did not run to freehand carving in hot wax.

If I may digress a moment, the really irritating part about this for me was that if we had been on dry land I knew exactly where I could go to obtain any seal I wanted, and probably some extra documents too. There was a certain monastery in northern France that I will not name where the monks had quite a business creating "15th century" charters for noblemen who wanted to prove that their families had always owned some plot of land or grand estate.

You might feel, as I did, that the involvement of religious bodies in forgery is morally questionable, but they explained to me that they made diligent enquiries before accepting a commission and would only agree to undertake the work if they believed that the person concerned had originally had a charter or other item that was lost, or could show their entitlement to such a document. That was all very well, but there was some evidence that their conviction of someone's right became much stronger if he left a purse of gold on the abbot's table.

Anyway, there I was somewhere on the North Sea and highly unlikely to find a monk skilled in forgery in the near future. Since there was nothing I could do about the seal at the moment I resolved to put it out of my mind for the remainder of the voyage, which I utterly failed to do.

Feeling the need for some fresh air I went aloft, or however sailors describe it, and took a short turn around the deck. More accurately, I grabbed the rail and climbed up to the little deck where Velders was standing, having noticed that the rail at the edge of the ship looked altogether too flimsy to stop me being launched into the icy water if the ship rolled suddenly.

'Master! Welcome!' said Velders, who was clearly such an experienced and accomplished sailor that he did not feel the need to tie himself to anything solid. 'Beautiful day, is it not?'

'It's rather breezy,' I said.

'It's fresh,' Velders conceded, 'but an excellent day for sailing. Look how the sails are filling.'

I glanced upwards briefly and resolved not to do that again.

'Would you like to take the helm?' Velders asked.

'Where do you want me to take it?' I replied.

'I mean, Master, would you like to steer the ship?'

'I don't think that would be wise. I've never steered a ship before.'

'Everyone has to start somewhere,' Velders laughed. 'Come, Master, young Wilkens here will give you a lesson. Don't worry, you won't hit anything. Can you see anything on the horizon?'

'No,' I confirmed.

'Well, it'll be the best part of an hour or more before we get as far as we can now see, so we need not worry about a collision. Just keep her steady as she goes.'

'What am I steering towards?' I asked.

'London, of course.'

'And how do I know where London is?'

'It's the way I've pointed the ship, more or less.'

I did not like the sound of that "more or less". 'But how do you know where London is in the absence of waymarkers?'

Velders laughed again. I would have said he was altogether too jolly to be a criminal, were it not that I've met several highly depraved individuals over the years who were extremely good company. 'I understand your concern, Master. It's very simple on a journey like this. We sailed from Hellevoetsluis along the coast to the south until we came to Walcheren. That sits on a similar latitude to London so if we sail due west from there, we'll find the mouth of the Thames.'

'You said "more or less". Why not "precisely"?'

'The wind may cause us to drift a little. We correct for that at night by navigating via the stars, which allows us to reset our course.'

Below me men were busily pulling on ropes and doing other nautical things.

'You have a lot of men here, Captain. How many are there in your crew?'

'For this trip we don't need too many. We're not expecting trouble and the men are not overly occupied. They are able to get some rest between watches, so we only have eighty.'

Eighty? And any one of them could, I suppose, have been responsible for the theft of my letter. Needless to say, many of them appeared to be illiterate, but maybe that was a cunning pretence adopted by men who did not want me to suspect them. I began to ponder whether a spy could have been insinuated into the crew by someone who knew of William's plan. The Stadhouder would have denied that anyone had knowledge of his intention, but he had been proved wrong before when those close to him had shown themselves to be untrustworthy.

I grasped the wheel as instructed and stared fixedly at the front end of the ship, since there was nothing on the horizon to steer towards, but then it dawned on me that even if I went hopelessly off course the pointy end would always be in front of me, at which juncture I began to panic. 'How do I know I'm going in the right direction?' I asked.

'If you don't move the wheel, you're going the right way,' said Velders, at which he tapped Wilkens on the shoulder and they both quitted the deck, leaving me in sole command of the ship.

I immediately thought of Acts, chapter twenty-seven, where we read "Paul comforted them, saying to them: Ye men, I see that the voyage beginneth to be with injury and much damage, not only of the lading and ship, but also of our lives." I have never thought that this was as comforting as the writer of Acts seemed to think. The only comfort I could take was that Velders' own life was at risk as much as mine, and he could not go far. Against that, it would only take a minute for a mighty storm to blow up with tragic consequences.

I called three or four times with increasing concern for Velders to return, which he finally did along with Wilkens. Both were red-faced with laughter at my expense.

'Forgive us, Master,' Velders said at length, 'it is just a pleasantry played on every man new to the sea. It was done to me in my turn.'

Retaliation is not a noble thought, but I made a mental note that if any accident befell Velders and I was compelled to preside at his funeral I would go so far and then throw the service book on his body and invite him to take over while I walked off, and see if he thought it such a capital joke then. Somehow it did not seem to carry quite the sting of his prank.

That night I curled up on my bed with the letter under my pillow and tried to sleep as the boat rocked in the wind, a sure sign that we were approaching the English coast. Sure enough, when I woke in the morning and glanced out I could see a thin sliver of land on the horizon. It looked quite sinister, as opposed to the Dutch coast which always appears friendly and welcoming.

'Another twelve hours and we should be tying up alongside in London,' said Velders cheerily.

'Twelve hours?' I shrieked. 'I can see England now. It's just there.'

'Indeed it is, Master, but it's around sixty miles from the mouth of the river to the City of London, and we won't make the speed we make in the open sea. Don't be surprised if we aren't there by nightfall, in which event I'll drop anchor somewhere and we can complete the journey tomorrow. It's a treacherous journey to make in the dark — unless, of course, you'd rather take the chance.'

'No, thank you. I'm in no hurry,' I replied. 'Take as long as you need.'

We were soon entering the Thames Estuary and passed the next few hours in one of the most crowded stretches of water on earth, sailing close enough to the bank to hear the abuse of patriotic Englishmen who seemed to think we were a very small invasion force.

Velders' prediction proved to be, if anything, an underestimate, and we dropped anchor in a wide part of the river for the night, resuming early the next day and finally docking in the City around eight o'clock.

My inclination to run ashore straightaway and throw the confounded letter at the first person I met had to be tempered. Velders' instructions were that we must call upon the Dutch ambassador to tell him what we were doing, at least in the most general terms. That is to say, we were to tell him what we were doing, but with some significant omissions, such as the real purpose of the exercise. It is not a good thing for ambassadors to be seen to be taking sides in what amounted to a civil war unless you are absolutely certain that you know who will win.

Our ambassador at the time was Aernout van Citters. Van Citters was a lawyer who had been sent to London about five years earlier and made himself thoroughly unpopular with English people of all social classes. In 1683 his carriage had been stoned by a mob who thought he was privy to the Rye House plot, about which I know next to nothing except that it involved attempting to kill King Charles II and his brother James after a race meeting and installing a Protestant king, and the ambassador's wife had been injured in the attack. Since James had come to the throne Van Citters had become equally hated by the ruling class who believed, rightly, that he was concerned that James was scheming to exclude his daughter Mary from the succession. James denied it, of course, but there were persistent rumours that he was planning to name a member of the French royal family as his successor. How fanciful these were I cannot say, but it was something of an obsession with Van Citters.

We called upon the ambassador who was out. This was ideal because we could leave our compliments without being subjected to any awkward questioning about things he might not want to know. I am not a diplomat, but I have come to realise that just because an ambassador says he wants to know everything the United Provinces is doing in his area does not mean he actually feels comfortable with knowing it. Sometimes it is convenient for them to be able to say that they know nothing about something or other, and I had a strong feeling that the fact that I had been told to tell Van Citters about the letter but not to give the letter to him to pass on to King James implied that Van Citters (and, by extension, William) would be in a very difficult position if the Duke of Monmouth's invasion were successful and the Duke discovered that William had tried to work against that outcome. Of course, there was the other possibility, which was that if an official source like Van Citters handed it over James would suspect that it was a trap and disregard it, which would actually be the worst possible outcome, because he might then move his troops to some positions that allowed Monmouth an unchallenged march to London.

I am not naturally a suspicious man. I like to see the best in people — even Englishmen — but as we walked through the streets of London I could not help but wonder what mischief Velders was up to. As the only person who knew about the letter he must have been responsible for its attempted theft, and I would have loved to know whether he had opened the letter he had succeeded in stealing and discovered that he had the wrong one. If so, I had to beware, because he might use violence on me to retrieve the correct one. I had the small penknife in my pouch but I doubt that would have deterred a determined attacker, even if I were quick enough to produce it while under threat.

Accordingly I resisted all temptations to take any shortcuts through alleyways and dithered about whether it was safer to keep Velders where I could see him or suggest we separated, in which event he might take the opportunity to lie in wait for me somewhere. I had nowhere safer than my person to keep the letter so I really wanted to lose it at the earliest possible moment, but if Velders were with me I dare not do so in case he picked it up.

What could his motivation be? I had started with the natural assumption that he was a supporter of the Duke of Monmouth, who wanted to prevent the disposition of his armies being known. That would be understandable if Velders were an ardent Protestant.

Suppose, however, that Velders happened to be a devout Catholic and thought the documents genuine. Might he try to steal the letter to give to James so as to ensure the King's success?

There was a third alternative, awful though it was. What if Velders' motivation was not religion, but money? Perhaps he had stolen the letter to sell it to the highest bidder. Given that Monmouth had sunk all his money into the expedition that presumably really meant in order to sell it to James, rather than giving it to him.

I was so engrossed in these convoluted thoughts that I absentmindedly stepped into a dung-heap and was obliged to rinse my boots at the nearest pump, a task not made any more pleasant by Velders' guffaws of laughter.

'My apologies, Master,' he chortled. 'If I had realised that you were going to walk through the manure instead of around it I would have warned you.'

It is not that we do not have manure in Dutch streets. Dutch horses are no better behaved in that respect than English ones. However, as soon as the horse is out of sight it is likely that some householder will appear with a spade and bucket to collect the free fertiliser and run home with it. One cannot look a gift horse in the end furthest from the mouth, as the proverb nearly has it.

'I must organise some provisions for the ship,' Velders suddenly announced. 'If I leave you alone will you undertake not to step or fall in anything unwholesome that you might tread around my clean ship?'

It was true that the *Nieuwpoort* was pristine, as befitted a Dutch ship — or, indeed, a Dutch anything — but that was largely because Velders had more sailors than he really needed for a trip to London and had set them to scrubbing the decks rather than sitting idle.

'I'll do my best,' I replied.

'It would be wise to be back on board by nightfall,' Velders added.

'On board? We're not lodging onshore?'

'Why pay for a bed when we already have one?' Velders asked.

Spoken like a true Dutchman, I thought. I wonder if he is one? True, I mean.

CHAPTER SIX

I found a nearby Catholic church and knelt in prayer. Just in case anyone saw me there I wrapped my cloak tightly round me to conceal my clothes, since a Reformed minister in a Catholic church might attract some comment.

I wanted to have a little chat with St Anthony, the patron saint of lost items. In the event that I managed to lose the letter I was supposed to leave behind, it would be good if St Anthony did not respond to anyone's prayer to help find it; but it also seemed to me that if anyone knew good places to lose things, it would be St Anthony. Were there particular areas of London from which he received a lot of prayers to find lost things, for example?

Needless to say, there was no response. I had not expected that there would be. This was not because I had any doubts about St Anthony's existence or powers, but because saints tend to answer prayers by actions rather than words. All being well, as I perambulated the city somewhere appropriate would recommend itself to me.

The first thought was that I did not want my letter picked up by the wrong class of person. Some illiterate barrow boy who would use it to light a fire, for example. Equally, I had to seek out a person who would immediately recognise its value to King James and who had the power to see that he got the letter.

The obvious person was King James' priest, but since he worshipped inside his palace it was hard to see how I could get it to him. There was no Roman Catholic bishop in London at that time who might have been another option. I also had to weigh the possibility that I would be recognised if I tried to sneak past the guards on the palace gates because I had been there eight years before; and since I had been partly responsible for the Queen's secretary being dismissed James had no reason to view me amicably.

But then I had a thought that should have occurred to me before. Didn't William say I was to meet the Bishop of Exeter and then lose the letter? Did that imply that I had to hang on to the wretched thing until I was about to leave the country?

This was depressing indeed. It extended the time during which I might be knocked on the head and thrown into a ditch considerably. The only advantage I could see in this arrangement was that I would be out of the country when it was found, so even if it was associated with me the English authorities would not be able to lay hands on me.

Before that happy day when I waved farewell to England, I hoped for the last time, I had to meet the Bishop of Exeter. Before I could do that, I had to be sent there by the Bishop of London; and before I could see the Bishop of London I had to have a conference with our ambassador to find out what he had arranged.

In the circumstances, my first move was obvious. I had to go to the ambassador's residence and wait until he showed up. At least I would be indoors, which was welcome since it had just started to rain.

If the maid was surprised to see me again so soon, perhaps that impressed upon her the urgency of my meeting with the ambassador. She allowed me to enter and wait in the hallway where a velvet-covered bench stood against the wall. This gave me an excellent view of anyone entering or, as it seemed at the time, ensured that I felt a blast of cold wind every time the door was opened.

After about twenty minutes the door was opened without a knock and a dark-haired gentleman entered, shaking off the rain and delivering himself of a torrent of Dutch which strongly suggested that he did not like the London weather. This could only be the ambassador, I thought, and sprang to my feet in anticipation.

The maid rushed forward to take the newcomer's cloak, in which action he assisted by throwing it over her as she approached. Since he was considerably larger in all directions than she was, the poor girl was soon hopelessly entangled. I lifted the cloak up so she could free her arms and gather it properly, after which she curtseyed to me very sweetly.

The dark-haired man wiped his nose with a handkerchief and eyed me with evident curiosity. 'A minister of religion, eh?'

'Yes, Ambassador. I am Master Mercurius of the University of Leiden.'

'Ah! The Stadhouder's emissary. Well, don't stand out there, man. Let us go into my study and find a fire to warm ourselves.'

Thrusting his hand out he shoved the door open and preceded me into a very pleasant and elegant room with high windows, beautiful wall decoration and a magnificent display of books. Unlike the Stadhouder's library, these looked as if someone had read them. Slips of paper poked out from several where the reader had wished to mark a page, and I would gladly have passed half an hour slowly perusing the shelves. It would have made up for the miserable day and the horrible sea voyage. In truth, I would gladly have crossed the sea to see these.

Without asking, the ambassador gave me a glass of wine. It was not a cup or horn beaker, but delicate Venetian glass. I immediately became convinced that I was about to drop it on the splendid rug, but the ambassador — a man of few words, it seemed — pointed to a chair and placed a small table at my elbow to receive the glass. In the interests of safety, I nudged the table forward a little so it was in front of me rather than beside me, thus ensuring that I would not forget that it was there when I got up.

My disquiet on this matter was the result of my innate clumsiness. My brother Laurentius was quite different. If pressed, he could have danced with a woman in full skirts amongst any number of tables without knocking one over. I, on the other hand, was capable of knocking over the only furniture in an otherwise empty room. I still blushed to think of the time twenty years earlier in France when I had somehow become trapped in a Confessional and dislodged the grille while trying to push the door open. It is surprising how much noise that makes in a large church.

The gentleman in front of me was Aernout van Citters, the ambassador of the United Provinces at the British court. Just to clarify, he was the son of Aernout van Citters and the father of Aernout van Citters, demonstrating better than any words of mine could that imagination was not the family's strong suit.

'I am glad that you have come, Master,' he said, standing with his back to the fire and raising his coat-tails to allow his posterior to thaw out. 'This country is in a ferment and our interests are in some jeopardy.'

'I will say frankly, Ambassador, that I am not a political animal. I shall have to rely in great measure on your assessment of the state of affairs here.'

This comment seemed to please Van Citters inordinately, and he proceeded to give me a lecture on the history of England since the turn of the century. Since I have already told you that, I will not repeat it here. Just accept that I told it better than he did. 'The situation is fraught with danger to us,' he continued. 'On the one hand, we have no great love of King James, who is a Catholic and well disposed to Louis of France. Against that, we have the Duke of Monmouth, a youth of some mettle but no great popular regard here. I cannot say how many would rally to his cause; but he is a Protestant, and that counts for much. There are some who would follow a dog if it were anti-Catholic. But then we must consider that if Monmouth gains the throne, our Princess Mary will never have it, and Monmouth, being but a bastard, has only a weak claim. Does the Stadhouder want to put himself in the position of appearing to overturn the established laws of succession, which could have unlooked for consequences?'

I knew what he was getting at. If you go around saying that there are circumstances in which the next in line does not automatically succeed to the throne, you put your own son in jeopardy. Not that William had a son; in fact, he never would, but he did not know that then.

Priests may not be the best people to appreciate this sort of argument, because generally we do not have sons and if we do, they rarely have any interest in succeeding us; and, of course, very few priests who have sons are brazen enough to advertise the fact and seek preferment for them. The obvious example of one who was is Pope Alexander VI, otherwise Rodrigo Borgia, who made his son Cesare a Cardinal. Since Cesare was only eighteen years old at the time, this was a doubly astonishing piece of cheek. Admittedly the young man had already accumulated three bishoprics as well as becoming Archbishop of Valencia, but it could hardly be said that he acquired any of these on merit, and he gave it all up five years later to become a soldier. You might think that going to war was much more perilous than being a leading light of the church, but during Alexander's pontificate some bad things happened to bishops and cardinals and being allowed to carry arms was probably a prudent move.

I realised belatedly that while I had been thinking these things Van Citters had continued to talk. Fortunately he did not appear to require any response from me, and by the time I gave him my full attention once more he seemed not to have advanced his arguments very far, so I doubt that I missed much.

'I have, at the urging of the Stadhouder, arranged for you to meet the Bishop of London privately. I will send to him now that you are here to fix a time. I assume that you are not otherwise engaged during your visit?'

I reviewed the things I could be doing in London, which largely meant casting my mind back to the activities of my last visit, and since having a sack thrown over my head and being kidnapped was not much fun I decided to forego that experience this time. 'No, Ambassador. I can attend upon the Bishop at his convenience.'

'You have already met him, I believe?'

'It is still Dr Compton, I think?' I asked.

'Indeed it is. A firm friend to the Reformed faith and a man who is well disposed to our country and our beloved Stadhouder.'

I had noticed that in those days people were falling over themselves with expressions of affection for the Stadhouder which, in many cases, had been notably lacking before he seized power; but, I suppose, if you are one of his ambassadors you can hardly be unenthusiastic about his rule.

A small boy was brought in by a maid. Since Van Citters addressed him in English, I assume that he was a local lad whom someone had recruited from a nearby street. The ambassador sat at his desk to write a note which he then folded and sealed. I did not see what he wrote but it cannot have been very lengthy.

'Here you are, boy,' Van Citters said. 'Take this to the Bishop's palace at Fulham — you know where that is?'

The boy nodded. Given the shiny coin in Van Citters' hand I suspect that he would have agreed even if he had no idea at all.

'If the Bishop is there, he may want you to bring a reply. Either way, come back here, and this shilling shall be yours.'

The boy was clearly spurred to great effort by the promise of such a reward, which was not surprising given that it represented about half a day's pay for a good workman, and I could see him through the window sprinting along the road.

'He won't keep up that pace,' observed Van Citters. 'It must be near on five miles to Fulham.'

Seen in that light, a shilling to run ten miles was not unreasonable.

'He will be a couple of hours, Master. Let us have a little refreshment and talk about our homeland. It will be a pleasure to be able to speak Dutch at length.'

Amen to that, I thought. Speaking English for a couple of hours would have been quite a challenge, even if I had the will to do so. I will not hide from the reader my view that English is a barbarous language with some horrible sounds. It required all my concentration to speak it.

We passed a pleasant time talking about Van Citters' time as a law student at Leiden where he graduated in 1655. That meant that his time overlapped briefly with my own though I had no recollection of him. Not only was his company enjoyable, but he sent to the kitchen for some food, and I am pleased to say that either he had a Dutch cook or he had trained an English one in proper cooking. It was as good a meal as I had experienced anywhere abroad, and I was feeling generally relaxed and at ease with the world when the door opened and the boy was readmitted.

He was, understandably, rather red in the face and fairly out of breath, but he stepped forward with his arm extended and clutching a letter of reply which Van Citters received with a word of thanks. Reaching into his waistcoat pocket he produced the shilling and pressed it into the lad's hand.

'You've done well, young fellow. Now, grab anything you can carry in your hand and take it to eat in the kitchen.'

The boy's eyes opened wide and he selected a leg of chicken, a patty and an orange.

'Watch him, Rose,' Van Citters said. 'Make sure he knows to peel the orange. He may never have seen one before.'

The maid bobbed in agreement and then chased after the young boy.

'Now,' said Van Citters, wielding a knife, 'let us see what the Bishop of London has to say.' He slit through the seal and unfolded the paper. 'Dr Compton sends his compliments,' he read, 'and looks forward to renewing your acquaintance.'

'It is kind of him to remember me.'

We had met eight years earlier when I was sent to London to assess the orthodoxy of Princess Mary's Protestant beliefs. I like to think that we got along very well.

'He asks if you are free now. There is no time like the present.'

'I suppose so. But how do I get there?'

'That is no problem. You can use my carriage. I'm not going out again today. My coachman can wait for you and take you back to your ship.'

'That would be greatly appreciated. You have been very helpful.'

Van Citters waved away my compliment. 'Nonsense. It is I who should be grateful to you. The interests of our nation require us to tread very carefully in the present circumstances. You have more freedom of movement than I do. We must keep in touch so we can plan our campaign together. Perhaps you would do me the kindness of visiting me again tomorrow? We dine at two in the afternoon.'

I gratefully accepted the invitation, and finished my wine as Van Citters went to give instructions to his coachman.

'The coach is waiting in the yard behind, Master. I trust you will not mind leaving by the back door?'

'Of course,' I said.

Since Van Citters had entered by the front door this struck me as a little strange, but I was only too grateful to avoid a five-mile walk, so I thanked him for his hospitality and took my leave of him.

The carriage was simply beautiful, painted a lustrous black with the lion of Nassau on each door in orange. I clambered inside and took my seat, reflecting, not for the first time, that a carriage is a wonderful mode of transport. I was, of course, very used to walking like everyone else, but being taken around the city in style was quite intoxicating. Thanks to the generosity of King Charles II and the Stadhouder, I had a little store of gold sufficient to allow me to buy and maintain a carriage, but I hesitate to think what my colleagues would have said if they had seen a humble lecturer in one. Besides which, I had nowhere to go most of the time, and Leiden is easier to navigate on foot.

The village of Fulham lies out to the south-west of the city by the side of the river, and is an area known for its market gardens. In fact, the general dampness and marshy nature of its environs reminded me forcibly of home, and as we passed along the High Road I could see field upon field of vegetables. One can readily understand why some of the great men of London choose to have their country homes here.

The Bishop of London lived in a large house surrounded by pleasant gardens and a moat, over which there was a drawbridge connecting him to the grounds of the nearby church. This building has a fine tower and, I was told, a set of bells unequalled in the kingdom, though I did not hear them rung myself. Beside the churchyard there was a handsome set of almshouses, then newly built, accommodating a dozen or so poor widows of which, sadly, there never seems to be a shortage.

We turned in at the gates and made our way to the door of the palace where Dr Compton was waiting to greet me. No doubt he was able to observe my approach from a side window as the carriage followed the sweeping arc of the driveway.

He advanced with a broad smile on his equally broad face, and greeted me effusively in Latin, the normal language of our discourse ever since he first heard me trying to speak English. I replied in like measure and after a few further pleasantries we entered his home while the coachman was directed to the stable-yard. I was to discover later that the Bishop's generous hospitality extended to plying my driver with copious amounts of ale, as a result of which the route back to the ship was convoluted in the extreme and nearly terminated in a ducking in the Thames, this calamity being avoided only by the good sense of the horses, who ignored the coachman's urgings and selected their own path along the river's margin.

But that is a story for later. For now, let me keep to the order of events, and resume my tale as I found myself in his library with a glass of excellent port wine and a plate of biscuits, as happy a circumstance as I had known for some time, especially when the Bishop excused himself to deal with some urgent matter and I was left alone with his books.

If only that moment could have lasted.

CHAPTER SEVEN

I love a good library.

There were books there that could well have induced me to break the Tenth Commandment by coveting them, and even one or two that would have put the Eighth Commandment — thou shalt not steal — into my mind.

I was just looking for a stool or ladder that would allow me to inspect the top shelf when Compton returned.

'Forgive me, Master,' he said cheerily. 'I spied the assistant gardener at work and thought that he was disregarding my instructions.'

'And was he?'

'No, he had merely failed to understand them; but it would have been equally injurious to the trees either way.'

He took his seat opposite me. 'I cannot tell you how delighted I was when I heard that the Stadhouder was sending you to London once more.'

I felt that I ought to say how delighted I was to be sent, but I am no good at lying.

'The situation is one of the utmost delicacy, Master,' the bishop continued. 'It is good to have a frank discussion so that I may know the Stadhouder's mind.'

That presupposed, of course, that I knew it myself, which may or may not have been true. I certainly knew what the Stadhouder had told me, but how much of that was for retelling to others I was not so sure about.

Equally, I was uncertain how far I could take the bishop into my confidence. I had no doubts, of course, about his honesty and integrity — and goodness knows there have not been

many I have met over a long life of whom I could say that —
but I had been mistaken before when it came to men's
motives; and in this case I use the word "men" to refer
exclusively to the male gender rather than as a general
appellation for mankind, because my ability to understand the
thoughts and motives of women was negligible. I could see
through my grandmother's increasingly transparent attempts to
marry me off to any woman who would have me, but
otherwise they have remained a glorious mystery to me.

I decided that before I committed myself to any definite view
I should find out what Compton was thinking. 'In the interests
of reciprocal clarity,' I began, 'may I ask how you find your
new King?'

Compton was a man known for his diplomacy and subtlety
of expression. 'He's a disaster,' he replied. 'Stubborn,
opinionated and usually catastrophically wrong. On top of
which, he is a Catholic and loses no opportunity to promote
the Catholic interest. That has become more important to him
than employing men of ability.'

'So the men I met a few years ago…?'

Compton tallied them on his fingers. 'Danby is at last
released from prison and back in Parliament.'

'I never met him,' I said, which was true, because Charles'
leading minister had absented himself from court while I was
last in London so that he could swear to the French
ambassador that he had no knowledge of a Dutch visit. Having
said that, his reputation was that he would not have scrupled at
a lie, especially if a purse of gold changed hands. However, he
had fallen from grace, accused of corruption. It was the talk of
Europe, especially in the court of Louis XIV, who was widely
believed to have engineered his downfall.

'Arlington is retired and spends much of his time on his estates. I doubt he would be in favour if he were at court but he withdrew himself when he found his influence waning. Sad to relate, he became a figure of mockery, much lampooned by our so-called wits.'

That was a shame. I had quite liked Arlington. Admittedly he had seriously hindered a murder inquiry I was working on, but he was very polite about it.

'And Mrs Paston?' I asked.

Compton's face fell. 'Oh, my dear Master; you have not heard.'

'Heard? Heard what?'

'I am sorry to say that the poor lady died last summer.'

I was shocked. She cannot have been much above thirty years old. Charlotte Paston was one of the King's Acknowledged Bastards, as she put it, and had been good company on my previous sojourn in London. I will not deny that she was, perhaps, a trifle forward by Dutch standards, but compared with many others in Charles' circle she was a paragon of restraint. For a start, she kept her clothes on in my presence, which is more than could be said for the Duchess of Portsmouth.

'And her husband?'

'Reputed to have converted to Catholicism.'

I jump ahead of my story, but some time after my visit Paston was made Treasurer of the Royal Household, a quite astonishing lapse of judgement by King James, since Paston's ability to deal prudently with money had been known to be negligible for years, and he was frequently separated from it at the gaming tables by men who did not even bother to cheat to do so.

I suppose that as a Catholic myself I should have rejoiced at this, but I found it very depressing. I doubt that Paston had the intellect to understand the doctrinal differences between Protestants and Catholics and if James was promoting such men it could only tend to advance the cause of the Duke of Monmouth. Many a Protestant would find himself forced into the Monmouth camp by James' actions.

'Does he understand the differences between the religions?' I asked.

'He understands that Catholics have the King's ear and Protestants do not,' Compton snapped.

'And do you, Bishop?'

Compton sighed. 'Not as before. I absent myself as much as possible, being too much associated by the King with the ministries of his late brother.'

'The pendulum will swing again,' I assured him.

'Perhaps. But to what avail if the clock be smashed to pieces while we wait?'

Compton refilled my glass. 'But tell me what brings you to England,' he said.

I hope that I will not be thought to be infirm of purpose if I say that I was uncertain how much to reveal. As I have said, I respected the Bishop's utter integrity, and was minded therefore to tell him about the stratagem of the forged letter; but if that ploy were to succeed, Compton needed to be as surprised as anyone else when the matter came up at court and the letter was revealed. Any hint that he was previously aware of it would place him in an awkward position and also imperil the success of the scheme. There were some people who might have pulled off this deception; the Princess Mary was regularly heard to exclaim "What a lovely surprise!" whenever she was presented with a bouquet of flowers, despite the fact that she received one at almost every engagement.

I decided, therefore, to give Dr Compton an abbreviated account of my mission; but, knowing him to be a sagacious and well-informed man, I would give him a full background, avoiding any mention of the letters.

'My mission is a delicate one,' I began. 'You will know, I expect, that the Duke of Monmouth is in exile in my country.'

'So I have heard.'

'I must tell you in the strictest confidence that the Duke is drafting plans for an invasion to remove King James and install himself as King.'

Compton smiled. 'There is no need for secrecy on that point, Master. The whole of London knows it. The only question is when and where he will strike.'

I took another sip of wine to collect my thoughts. 'You will understand that my master the Stadhouder is ambivalent about the Duke's mission.'

'One can understand why,' Compton replied. 'If the Duke becomes King there is no prospect of our dear Princess Mary becoming Queen.'

'Quite so.'

'So will William support the Duke's uprising? The talk here is that he will allow the Duke to do all the hard work and then invade himself to snatch the kingdom back, proclaiming Mary as the rightful heir and encouraging Englishmen to rise up against the usurper.'

This possibility had not occurred to me. Surely William would not be so duplicitous? Actually, he probably would, I decided, if he felt it necessary; but from William's point of view, restraining the Duke had an additional benefit. If James died and Mary inherited there was a risk that the Duke would then try to seize the crown on the basis that Mary was a woman, so there would be every reason for the English to fall in with William's plan to have himself declared joint monarch. While he loved the United Provinces, and enjoyed being a Stadhouder, it was not the same as being a king. I just hoped that if his plan succeeded he forgot all about me, because I had no desire to flit back and forth across the North Sea.

'I do not think that is very likely,' I told Compton, picking my words very carefully. 'I have been sent here to gauge the degree of support that the Duke has, in the hope that if it is low, he can be dissuaded from fruitless loss of blood, and if it is high, that King James can be induced to retire so as to avoid carnage.'

'Amen to that!' exclaimed Compton fervently. 'We do not need another civil war. I lost my father in the last, and do not mean to risk my nephew in any recurrence.'

Compton's father was the Earl of Northampton, which, to my bafflement, appears to be nowhere near Southampton. How anyone is meant to find their way around this wretched country is beyond me. The Earl was killed in battle; a touching story tells how his horse was surrounded by Parliamentary infantry and he was invited to surrender to spare his life, but refused, saying that he scorned quarter from such base rogues, which was a pretty speech but did nothing to prevent his being clubbed to death. I could imagine the Bishop saying something like that in those circumstances.

The Bishop's nephew, George, was now the Earl, though barely come to manhood. I know all this only because Dr Compton explained it to me as we sat, but I have condensed his account so as not to weary the reader.

[Marginal note: Van der Meer had a coughing fit at this point. Sometimes I fear he forgets who feeds and clothes him.

There are other clerks who would be glad of this work, and some of them will be better spellers.]

Compton pressed me to have a little supper with him, and when I was on the point of declining out of consideration for the poor coachman who brought me there, he assured me that the man would be well refreshed too. I did not realise that this would be largely consumed in liquid form, which may explain the bizarre route we took afterwards. Some day I must look up where Chiswick is on a map, because I am fairly certain we should never have passed through there on the way to my ship.

'May I ask, Dr Compton, whether you think the Duke's cause is popular?' I enquired as we sat down.

Dr Compton waited until the servants had left us before replying. 'It is hard to say, Master. No man will declare himself in the present troubling times. On the one hand, the King is not much favoured by the common people, but he is the anointed King, which counts for much with them. And we are enjoying some peace and prosperity. One must not forget, either, that King James played a major part in combatting the great fire here near twenty years ago, and is loved by the merchants of the city on that account.'

Readers who have enjoyed the previous volume of my memoirs [Yes, Van der Meer, I chose the word *enjoyed* deliberately] may recall that I met some merchants in Amsterdam, a self-serving and arrogant bunch, so I was as sure as any man could be that these rich boys would stop at nothing to keep James on the throne if they thought it would be profitable.

'And you, Your Grace; may I ask what you think?'

Compton absently picked some meat from a chop. 'I think James to be a poor King; but I do not know that the Duke will be a better one. I place my hopes on the Princess Mary, whom

I esteem greatly as a young woman of sense, and on her husband, who seems to me to be an honest and tolerant leader.'

Since Compton had been one of Mary's tutors, he had enjoyed plenty of opportunity to assess her merits. As for those of my master, honesty and tolerance were indeed two of his finer qualities. If I had been asked to extend the list much I might have struggled, but I could not argue with those.

'I take it, then, that if the Duke invaded he could not count on your support.'

'I doubt that my support would make any difference one way or the other,' Compton laughed. 'But at present I would say that the City of London will oppose him, as will those who have been raised to high office by the King. The matter will turn on whether he can garner support among the common people. He would be well advised, if he comes at all, to land in some distant place and test his following among the people there, so that he may withdraw in safety if he finds them unwilling to serve him.'

I almost wondered whether Compton had seen the so-called secret plans that I had, except that they were safely stowed inside my shirt.

'I guess, Master, that this is why I have been asked to introduce you to the Bishop of Exeter?'

I hesitated, largely because I did not know whether the answer was yes or no, but I was spared the need for any comment by Dr Compton, who did not wait for one, but smiled and continued.

'The Bishop, Dr Thomas Lamplugh, is well on in years — near seventy, I think — and a man of some learning. Like many old men, he is averse to change. And he has a suspicious nature. He sees plots everywhere because he is a great plotter himself.'

He and William of Orange would get along famously, then, I thought, but said nothing.

'Somehow,' Compton continued, 'he has contrived to be simultaneously Bishop of Exeter and Dean of Rochester.'

'Surely,' I ventured hesitantly, 'Exeter is a long way from Rochester?'

'Exeter is a long way from everywhere, which is one reason why Dr Lamplugh likes to live in London as much as he can, but at present he is in Exeter, I believe. I have written to him to say that you will be visiting and that I should welcome his opinion on certain weighty matters, but I have not told him what they are.'

'And will you welcome that opinion?' I asked.

'Of course not. But it will flatter him to think that I might.'

Full of good food and wine I flopped back in the luxurious seat of the ambassador's carriage, and so began my mystery tour of London in the grip of a coachman who had been generously plied with ale. Our circuitous route gave me plenty of opportunity for thinking.

At last my plan seemed to be coming together. I would dine with the ambassador on the following afternoon, set out on the next tide for Exeter, meet the Bishop thereof at the earliest opportunity, and waste no time before divesting myself of my secret letter. I would then ask a few questions about the defences of Exeter to raise people's suspicions that the letter might be genuine, return to my ship and pray that the winds were favourable and we could make all speed to return us to the comfort and security of my native land. Upon docking I would proceed at once to the Binnenhof, report to the

Stadhouder and then return to my books, resolved never to be employed by great men again. Even the prospect of teaching undergraduates took on a rosy glow, because occasionally I met one of real promise. It had happened in 1668, 1675 and I was about due another one.

Little did I know that even then my plan had begun to unravel.

CHAPTER EIGHT

The coachman drew up at ship after ship looking for the *Nieuwpoort* before finally locating it in precisely the place where I had left it. I slipped a piece of silver in his hand, begging that he would take great care in returning to the ambassador's house, since I was by no means confident that he could remember where it was or find it if he did, and the Thames is very treacherous for those who try to drive carriages across it without using a bridge. The coachman touched his hat and shook the reins, and the horses drew away. I had considerably more faith in their ability to find their own stable than I had in the coachman to direct them there, and determined that I should ask the ambassador the next afternoon whether he had ever seen his carriage again.

I boarded the boat, not without some trepidation at walking along a wet plank, and was immediately hailed by someone who inspected me closely by the light of a lantern.

'Ah, it's you, Master,' came a voice out of the darkness, and the lantern was moved so I could see its bearer.

'Wilkens? Good evening.'

'Good evening, Master. I hope you've had a successful day.'

'Yes, thank you, I think I have.'

'Captain Velders isn't with you, Master?'

'No. Should he be?'

'It was just that you left together, so I thought he might be with you.'

'He left me quite quickly, saying that he had to arrange some fresh supplies for the ship.'

Wilkens looked concerned. 'Nothing has been delivered, Master. And Captain Velders hasn't returned to the ship yet.'

'I see. That's concerning. What does Lieutenant Hendriks suggest?'

Wilkens looked unhappily at me. 'I don't know, Master. He hasn't returned either.'

I am prepared to admit that my reaction was not as compassionate as it might have been. 'Do you know how to sail this ship, Wilkens?' I asked.

'Yes, Master, but I can't do it single-handed. It's not the sailing that worries me. It's trying to navigate.'

This last problem seemed to have a fairly straightforward answer in my eyes. If we left the mouth of the Thames and just kept going I didn't see how we could miss the continent of Europe. We would eventually find landfall somewhere, and once we did I could make my way back to Leiden, on foot if necessary. I enjoy a good walk.

'Perhaps we might find a suitable navigator in London,' I suggested.

'There must be men who could serve,' Wilkens agreed, 'but very few who will consent to do so without payment, and I do not have a key to the captain's chest. The captain has one, and the lieutenant has the other.'

This all smacked to me of a shocking lack of foresight. How could the only people with keys be allowed to go missing simultaneously? 'Does this mean that the sailors won't get their pay?' I asked. 'Surely that will give rise to some discontent?'

'Master, sailors are well used to not being paid on time. But as it happens, they have no need of money until they return to Hellevoetsluis, where they will be paid.'

'What about purchases in England?'

'They are not allowed off the ship, Master. None of us are. Only the captain and lieutenant may go ashore.'

'At the same time?'

Wilkens looked uncomfortable. 'That would be very unusual, Master. Normally one or other of them must be here to ensure the security of the ship.'

I was perplexed. 'I understand why Captain Velders went ashore, Wilkens; and presumably he explained his plan to Lieutenant Hendriks. So when and why did Hendriks leave?'

'I cannot be sure, Master. None of us saw him leave. But it can surely only have been for the most important cause that he would desert his ship in this way.'

'Indeed. Well, let us hope that he returns soon and can enlighten us as to why he had to go so suddenly.'

Wilkens suddenly looked both acutely unhappy and remarkably young. He looked at me with the sad eyes one might have expected from a child of five or six. 'Master, what do you think we should do?'

'Do? I don't know. Presumably you're the officer in charge now, since you're the only officer.'

With the benefit of hindsight I can see that this was, perhaps, not the most tactful way of describing our current situation. At any rate, Wilkens did something rather unexpected in an officer of the Dutch Navy. He began to cry.

'What is it?' I asked, as solicitously as I could given a sudden urgent need to make water.

'I've only been an officer since the day before we left,' he replied. 'I was a cadet before. And since I don't know what our mission is, I don't know how to carry it out. Oh, I hope the captain and lieutenant return soon!'

I hate to see a grown man cry. It is likely to set me off too, and I could already feel tears welling in my eyes. 'Let me briefly go to my cabin and then I will return here and we will discuss what can be done.'

'Thank you, Master. It's just that, as the Stadhouder's representative, we all look up to you.'

I acknowledged the compliment with a cursory nod before rushing below, finding the nearest chamber pot, and attending to my comfort. I then splashed my face with water to help me think more clearly, and returned to the deck. Wilkens was resting his head on the rail of the little raised deck at the back of the ship.

'Are you quite well?' I enquired.

Wilkens lifted his unhappy face towards me. 'Sorry, Master. I've been on watch for fifteen hours now. I'm very tired.'

'That's appalling. I shall have strong words with Velders and Hendriks when they return.'

'I don't mind, Master, if only they come back soon.'

'Well, what exactly are you doing here?' I asked.

'I watch for anyone attempting to enter or leave the ship without authority, Master.'

'I see. Surely anyone can keep watch?'

'It's my responsibility as the senior officer on board. Then I have to watch for anyone attempting to damage the ship.'

'Why should anyone do that?'

'It isn't that long ago that we were at war with the English, Master. It wouldn't surprise us if someone started a fire or cut the mooring ropes.'

'And if you saw someone, how would you stop them? There might be a mob.'

'We have guns and swords, Master. I'd need the whole crew mustered, though. That's why they're not allowed to go ashore.'

We stood in silence for a few moments, gazing at the dockside and the inviting lights of nearby taverns, before I decided to open my mouth and jam my foot in it.

'I can watch the ship for you. You go and get some sleep. I can always send for you if anything happens.'

Wilkens' eyes lit up. 'Would you, Master? That's very kind of you.'

He did not attempt to dissuade me, but doffed his hat and ran to the stairs down to the cabins, and I found myself on the deck with nothing to occupy me. It had crossed my mind that I might read a book, if I had one, and if it were light enough, which it wasn't. Instead I decided to keep warm by walking the length of the deck. Well, not quite the whole length; prudence dictated that I kept at least two paces from the edge at all times.

After my fiftieth lap I was beginning to regret my impetuous decision. I had completely failed to obtain any assurance that Wilkens would return. Suppose he met with some accident? I would be in charge of a ship, not only unsuited to command, but totally ignorant about how to sail the thing. Not only that, I could not give an order in language the men would understand.

Fortunately all was quiet, so I found myself a ledge to sit on and decided to devote the night hours to considering the mission thus far.

On the plus side, I still had the letter. On the minus side, I had lost two officers and my diplomatic accreditation, and if I went ashore as planned in the morning — without any sleep, mark you — and then returned to the ship for the evening tide — and who knew when that was going to be? — I would be in the difficult position of not having anyone who could aim the vessel in the direction of Exeter. Perhaps if I asked the ambassador nicely he might find a Dutch ship's master who could be trusted to convey me to that city which, cursory inspection of a map had revealed, was perilously close to the Atlantic Ocean. If we sailed past it we might find ourselves adrift for weeks before we found the Americas; *if* we found the Americas, that is. I began to wish that I had paid more attention in geography lessons.

I wrapped myself in my cloak and stared into the darkness. The boat rocked slowly on the waves and I began to feel my eyelids growing heavy. I fought to stay awake, and seemed to be winning the battle when my attention was drawn to a loud noise.

A moment's reflection proved that it had been caused by my head hitting the deck. I must have dropped off my ledge, and I would have sworn that only a second or two had passed, were it not for the fact that I could see dawn breaking in the distance.

My tiredness may have been eased by my brief nap, but I assure the reader that nothing causes a man to wake up more than the thought that his ship may have been cut adrift or burned to the ground while he slept. [Yes, Van der Meer, I realise that a ship isn't on the ground, but I can't think of a better expression at the moment. Make a note and we'll come back to it.]

As it happened, neither of these things had occurred, allowing me to regain my composure, though not before a malodorous seaman sidled up to me in the gloom and spoke to me in the most uncivil terms.

'I trust Your Honour enjoyed his little sleep on watch,' he gurgled. 'Of course, if any of us done that we'd get the lash. But I s'pose there's no harm done, you being a gentleman.'

He held out a hand, the clear implication being that his silence about my little dereliction could be purchased at a price. I had no idea what the going rate for such bribes was, never having been blackmailed before, and fished in my pouch for a suitable coin. It was difficult to tell them apart in the dawn light, and I barely had time to register that it was a guilder before it was snatched from my grasp by the blackguard, who touched his cap in salute.

'Bless 'ee, Master, for an open-handed gentleman! And the very soul of diligence, for hadn't we Your Honour's eye upon us the whole night long!' So saying, he broke into a grin which nearly split his beard in two and gave me the largest of winks before running off to stow his bounty somewhere.

I had time for a couple of hours' sleep before taking my breakfast, and as I arrived at the table I was surprised to find Hendriks there.

'Lieutenant! You're back!' I said.

Hendriks looked bewildered. 'Where else would I be?'

'We feared some harm must have befallen you when you had not returned. Poor Wilkens had to serve a double watch.'

'I have apologised for that. I expected the captain to be here. But I did return in time for my own shift.'

'And you have no idea where Captain Velders is?'

'I thought he went with you, Master. His business was not my business.'

'And what was your business?'

Hendriks looked offended by my impertinent question, but must have decided that an account was necessary, given the captain's disappearance. 'I had a letter to deliver, Master, then I decided to see the famous Covent Garden.'

There was something about his expression that suggested to me that the attraction, whatever it was, cannot have been the vegetable market.

'Did you find anything of interest there?' I asked, as levelly as I could.

'A very sweet young lady who consented to accompany me to dinner and show me some of the sights.'

I did not need to ask which sights those were. [Van der Meer sniggered here. He obviously did not need to ask either.] 'And are you not concerned at the possibility of disease, Lieutenant?' I asked.

'No, Master, because I have one of these.'

He produced a sort of little sack of fine leather and it was a moment or two before I worked out what a man does with it.

'I'm sorry, Master,' he continued. 'I did not realise that you would be embarrassed.'

'I'm not embarrassed,' I stammered, despite the fact that I could feel the burning in my cheeks. 'Anyway, shouldn't you wash it?'

'I suppose so,' he said. 'It hadn't occurred to me. You don't think it might weaken the leather?'

'I have absolutely no idea,' I snapped, 'but I imagine that a lady would wish to be assured that it had been washed since its last use.'

Hendriks seemed genuinely perplexed. 'They've never mentioned it,' he answered, 'but if you think it's advisable…'

What I actually thought was that the sinful object should be immediately incinerated. Never before had I seen such an incitement to vice. I was also rather shocked that Hendriks should have been disporting himself in such a manner at a time when his commander was missing.

Except, of course, that he had at that time no way of knowing that Velders had disappeared. After all, I had left at the same time as Velders and I had not known, or I should not have spent time enjoying myself in Fulham. This is not to disparage the Bishop of London's company, you understand; but I could not have been at ease knowing that my mission had been so thoroughly imperilled. We had to find Velders. I suppose that Hendriks and Wilkens between them could probably find Exeter and sail home, but I did not relish returning to The Hague to tell the Stadhouder that we had lost the man that he had personally selected to command the *Nieuwpoort*. He would probably want to take it out of my pay, though come to think of it he had not offered me any. That was not unusual. William seemed to think it was the duty of every true Dutchman to offer him his services free of charge, or, at least, that was the attitude that he took with me; not that he had not proved generous after the event, once I had survived. I suppose that if any of the murderous attacks on me had succeeded he would have deeply regretted paying anything up front.

Needless to say, the notion that we had to find Velders was easy to express but hard to achieve. London is a very large city. Despite the famous fire, there remained a great many alleyways and it was relatively easy to travel to the outlying villages like Fulham, Islington and Tooting, to name but three I had heard mentioned. Whatever wickedness the captain was up to, I had no doubt that he would have hidden his tracks well, and it is no easy matter to find someone who does not wish to be found.

That led to the question of what manner of wickedness he had in mind. Let us suppose that he had not looked at the letter he stole from me. No doubt he had hoped to sell it to either the King or to someone sympathetic to the Duke of Monmouth who would not wish it to fall into the wrong hands; and it was reasonable to assume that he had some names in mind before he stole it. It was possible that he acted out of conviction rather than avarice, and sincerely believed that the victory of one or other party was a good thing in itself; but a man who steals his master's correspondence is ruining his future prospects of employment, for which man of sense will employ a known deceiver or common thief? It might be that he hoped for some reward from the recipient, but it was unlikely to compensate for the loss of all employment, not to mention the serious damage to his reputation.

Taking all this together, it was surely more probable that he would try to sell it for ready money; in which event I could see one of two outcomes. He might succeed, but then he would face an angry customer once the letter had been opened and revealed not to be as described, or it might have been opened before sale, which might cause him a lot of face but was probably safer for him. I have no experience of this sort of thing, but it seems likely that a man who had revealed themselves to be a traitor by offering to buy a secret missive might not take it too well to find it was nothing of the kind.

As to what had happened to Captain Velders, this analysis suggested two incompatible outcomes. He might have succeeded and be on the run with his ill-gotten gains, when common prudence suggested he would get out of London as soon as possible and never be seen again; or he might have failed, in which case we could reasonably expect to find him lying in a ditch somewhere.

And if Velders had been ill-used in this way, when he did not actually have the letter, what might happen to me if anyone discovered that I had it? It did not bear thinking about. I am not cut from the cloth of martyrs. I always hoped to die in a comfortable bed, not in an alleyway in a foreign land, especially not this one, where I was an unwilling visitor in the first place.

Is it morbid to wonder when and where you will die? It first pressed upon me when my brother Laurentius was killed at sea during the Battle of Lowestoft. How unprepared must a man be when all his thoughts must be directed towards his duty? How can any soldier or sailor give attention to the condition of their immortal soul when the bullets fly about their ears?

But then I thought of my cousin Margriet. When I was first at the University she lived about an hour's walk from my home village. I do not remember her well, for she was three or four years older than me, our mothers being sisters; a vivacious girl, not long married, and in excellent health. I journeyed home at the end of my first year as a student to receive the melancholy news of her death in childbirth, the infant too having succumbed.

It will not surprise the reader that a man who was, in large part, brought up by his mother and grandmother should feel some warmth and sympathy for the lot of women. How must they feel to know that an act of love may, within a year, lead to their untimely death? They expose themselves to sacrifice each time they are brought to the birthing bed, and what fears must trouble their breasts at such a moment? I recall my grandmother telling me that every woman knew a friend who had perished in childbirth. Whatever the natural inclinations of a man, the possibility that I might cause the passing of a woman dear to me was a powerful buttress to my celibacy.

I shuddered. If my participation in one of William's "little jobs" had been unwilling hitherto, it was now a definite disinclination. I would count the days until I stood on Dutch soil again. It even crossed my mind that if I messed up my assignment it would protect me against being given any other in the future, but I knew I could not do it. I must give my best efforts, though I paid for my diligence.

A clock somewhere struck ten o'clock. It was rather early in the morning to start drinking genever, but the temptation was very great. However, that way ruin lies, so I did the next best thing, and found a church to pray in.

CHAPTER NINE

Sometimes ordinary men and women suppose that those of us who are ordained have some special right of audience that ensures that our prayers are lifted to the front of God's list. If only it were so; there are times when I think He is barely listening at all to me, though I know as an article of faith that He does, and that our prayers are answered. It is just that sometimes when God speaks to me, He whispers, and if I am not paying attention I might not hear Him at all.

It was not so on this particular morning. As I knelt in the cool interior of a church I prayed fervently. It was said of Our Lord that He prayed so hard in the Garden of Gethsemane that the sweat fell like blood from Him as He asked God to let the cup of suffering pass from Him.

I cannot say I had quite so much to worry about, but I prayed no less intensely that I would do my work satisfactorily, return to Leiden, and there become entirely invisible to Stadhouders until I died at a great age in my bed. Naturally I concluded my prayer as we always must, saying 'Yet not my will, but Thine be done.' I just hoped that the Almighty would adjust His plans to make these things happen.

As I knelt there I had a strange sense that God was speaking to me. Words formed in my head that I was not putting there, and they seemed entirely appropriate to my condition.

Stop moaning, said God, *or I'll give you something to moan about.*

I will not deny that I was rather taken aback by this directness, so much so that I started and wobbled on my knees, but I recovered myself, genuflected (after looking about me to ensure that I was not being observed), picked up my hat and made to leave.

My way was barred by a small woman with weathered skin and a basket containing some kind of herb. She spoke to me, but I did not comprehend her, so she tried again, louder and slower, as the English do when faced with a foreigner.

'Will you buy a lucky posy from a Romany woman, sir?' she asked.

I had not previously encountered them but I believe her to have been what the Greeks call *tsinganoi* and we know in Dutch as zigeuner.

I hesitated, which she took to be a refusal, and therefore attempted a different sale.

'I'll read Your Honour's palm, if it please you.' Without waiting for an answer she grabbed my arm and turned the hand palm upwards. 'Ah! A long life ahead of you, sir,' she announced. Well, she was right about that one. 'A long journey in prospect too,' she continued. That was hardly surprising, given that I was evidently not English. 'And one with peril lurking in it,' the old crone wittered on.

I hoped she was wrong about that. I had been wishing that she was going to look into my future and declare that nothing was going to happen in my life except for some long hours in a library and a tankard of ale now and again; though I did hear of a fellow who was seriously hurt when he pulled a bookshelf over on top of himself in a library in Germany. Of course, German words are longer than ours and some of their theological works are extremely ponderous, so it is no surprise that the accident had terrible consequences.

I tried to withdraw my hand but she held it tenaciously, so much so that I could not give her a copper or two to conclude the transaction.

'You are too trusting, sir. You'll be betrayed if you're not careful. But in adversity you will find a true friend.'

This species of general piffle could, of course, mean anything and nothing, but having delivered herself of it the old woman seemed to consider her performance done, so I dipped into my pouch to find a coin for her. I gave her a couple of small coins, whereupon she insisted upon tucking a sprig of herb in the band of my hat.

'God go with you, sir,' she said cheerfully.

'And with you,' I returned automatically.

'I don't need His company like you do, sir,' she replied.

Somewhat unnerved by this pronouncement I stumbled out into the daylight, or what would have been daylight had it not been raining. When I was small my grandmother used to tell me that rain was the tears of angels. I doubt that this was true, but if it was I can only suppose that some event of the most distressing kind must have taken place in Heaven, because the angels were bawling their eyes out. The English, of course, are very used to this, and simply went about their usual business, some of them even pausing while running across the streets to tell their acquaintances how awful the weather was, whereas I made my way along the road doorway by doorway.

To my delight I found a bookshop and loitered there for a while. There was a book by an Englishman named Bunyan, entitled *The Pilgrim's Progress*, that I should have liked to have bought but I could not carry it with me; but, observing my indecision, the bookseller undertook to deliver it to my lodgings. Fearing that, if he delayed the ship might have already sailed, I suggested instead that it might be carried to the ambassador's house, which the fellow undertook to do if I paid for the book in advance; which I did, thanking him for his kindness and hoping that my English was good enough to comprehend it entirely.

Thus enlivened by the prospect of a new book, I stepped out to find that the rain had ceased for a while — rain always ceases "for a while" in England, for there always seems to be another shower in prospect — and continued on my way to dine with the ambassador.

Van Citters was pleased to see me again, and after a little pleasant conversation we repaired to the dining-room to enjoy a sumptuous dinner, during which my book arrived. I usually eat sparingly, largely because the food in the refectory at the University is prepared by Albrecht, the kitchen master, a culinary pyromaniac if ever there was one, but on this occasion I found the food very much to my taste.

'I understand that the Bishop of London has sent to the Bishop of Exeter on your behalf,' Van Citters announced.

'So I believe, Ambassador. I had been hoping that we might set out this evening, but I understand that the ship's captain has gone missing.'

'Missing?'

'Yes, he went ashore yesterday and did not return in the evening.'

I said nothing about the missing letter. The fewer people who knew about that, the better. I suppose that the ambassador might have furnished me with another, but why would he, if I am going to go around losing them?

'That is unusual,' said Van Citters. 'I can understand a man wishing to look around a city on his travels, but I should have expected the master of a ship to exercise more responsibility than to sleep ashore without warning. Has he returned yet?'

'Not when I left this morning. But that was some hours ago. He may have reappeared by now. I shall let him have a piece of my mind when I see him. He could have imperilled the whole mission.'

'Indeed,' Van Citters remarked. 'It is a task of some delicacy too, is it not? It would be catastrophic if your letter were prevented from reaching its intended recipient.' He took a bite from an apple and chuckled heartily. 'Imagine how terrible it would be if you lost it!'

I forced a feeble laugh to show that I appreciated the irony, though I cannot say that I found the idea as amusing as Van Citters evidently did.

The ambassador pressed some more wine on me. 'Come, Master, be of good cheer! No doubt when you return to the ship the good captain will be at his post making everything ready for your departure.'

'I suppose so. I ought to be thinking about getting back. I wouldn't want to be the cause of any delay.'

There came a knock at the door followed by some discussion between the maid and whoever had been admitted. The maid seemed to be telling whoever it was that the ambassador was not to be disturbed, but the visitor was persistent. At length Van Citters went to see what the fuss was about.

'What is so urgent?' he demanded.

The visitor was a man in a dark blue coat, sober of appearance. I took him for a minor official of some kind.

'I apologise for disturbing you, Your Excellency,' the man began, 'but I have been to St Bartholomew's Hospital. They have a man there who is in a bad case, having been set upon by footpads. He appears, from certain papers found upon his person, to be one of your countrymen, and the surgeon thought that you should be informed.'

Van Citters looked at me enquiringly. 'Could it be Captain Velders?' he asked.

'There is only one way to find out,' I replied, taking up my hat and hurriedly drinking the last of the ambassador's wine.

The ambassador's carriage was quickly made ready, and the three of us clambered aboard. The coachman was ordered to maintain his normal pace so as not to draw attention to us. Given the pace of the other horses in London, this was a safer option too.

The city of London maintains some hospitals at public expense and it was to one of these that the Dutchman had been taken. This institution was above five hundred years old and parts of the buildings were not in good condition; but that it existed at all for the relief and comfort of the poor and elderly was greatly to the credit of Londoners.

We were led by a porter to a pallet where the injured man lay. His head was swathed in bandages and was wedged between two bolsters, so that we could not immediately see his face. Given the status of the ambassador, the superintendent and chief surgeon of the hospital were summoned to speak with us.

'How is he?' asked Van Citters.

'He fares tolerably well,' announced the surgeon, 'inasmuch as we expected him to die swiftly from the terrible wounds to his skull. Whether he will ever wake again is in the hands of God.'

'Is it possible to see his face?' I asked.

The surgeon considered this for a moment. 'His head is fixed in this position so that he will not roll over onto the fractured skull. It was necessary to open the scalp and prise the bony sections of skull out of his brain, where the continued bleeding was causing pressure that could only be injurious to the delicate structures beneath. It was not possible to return all the pieces of skull to their former position, as a result of which a part of his brain is unprotected. However, if you will come to this side, I will support the head while my assistant removes the bolster. I pray that you will be as quick as possible so that we may return him to his supported state as soon as may be.'

I assented and dropped to my knees so that my face was level with his. The surgeon carefully inserted his hand under the victim's cheek, placed the other on the uppermost ear, and nodded, whereupon the bolster was removed briefly, and I found myself looking at the battered face of Captain Velders.

There is a brief hiatus in the story at this point because I cannot recount what happened next, except to say that when I next had possession of my faculties I was coughing due to the proximity of some foul salts under my nose while the surgeon poured me a glass of rum from a flask in his pocket.

'It should be brandy,' he declared to the ambassador, 'but we have none. If the inmates suspected that there were spirituous liquors about the place that door would long since have been demolished.'

'What happened?' I mumbled.

'You fainted,' said Van Citters.

'An episode of syncope,' the surgeon explained.

'Which means...?' I asked.

'You fainted,' the surgeon said. 'Clean as a whistle. One minute, on your knees, the next — bonk! Let me look at your cheek there.' He carefully probed it with his fingers. 'Nothing broken, but you'll have a fine bruise in the morning.' He turned to one of the porters. 'Madeley, have we a beefsteak for the Master?'

'Thank you, I'm not hungry,' I said.

'It's not to eat. It's to place on the bruise.'

This sounded to me like an utter waste of good beefsteak, as surely as if it had been given to Albrecht to cook, but I have made enquiries since, and it appears to be general medical practice. I have no idea why it should work, or why meat should work better than, say, a herring or a cabbage, but then I am not medically qualified. Having said that, a lot of the remedies adopted by medical men are identical with those practised by my grandmother, so why they need five years of study when they could just ask some passing old crone is not clear to me. Admittedly my grandmother also espoused a selection of remedies that are definitely not mainstream medical thought, such as placing a toad on your chest if you had hiccups, and she had some ideas about means for promoting the conception of twins that are perhaps best not committed to paper, but the reader will understand the drift of my argument.

I am not familiar with rum, and after my first taste of it I resolved not to bother again. It gave me a warm feeling within, and a strong sense that my ribs had just been kicked by a donkey, but the main advantage it bestowed on me was a clear sense of the first thing that I had to do. I needed to retrieve my letter if I possibly could.

'Do you still have his clothes?' I asked.

This question seemed to stir some degree of consternation, but when Madeley returned with a small piece of steak he was able to confirm that Velders' clothes were safely stowed in the large press behind us. In no time he had produced a basket in which Velders' outer clothes were neatly folded or rolled.

'Was there no sword?' I asked.

'I put it aside in the lockable pantry,' Madeley remarked. 'It was too fine to risk it being stolen or lost.'

Here was my first puzzle. What sort of footpad attacks a man with a club or staff when he can see that the victim has a sword and, presumably, knows how to use it? I could only imagine that the attack was made from behind, and that the perpetrator was relying heavily on the element of surprise.

'Is it your opinion, Doctor, that Captain Velders was struck from behind?'

'It is not impossible, but more likely that he was facing his assailant. The nose and cheeks were severely battered, whereas the back of the head is largely intact. But he might, I suppose, have received one blow from behind and then a volley from above as he lay on the ground.'

I could not picture that. If a man is struck from behind, surely he falls face down? He might, I suppose, roll over given time, but if he has time for that would he not draw a weapon first? 'Are his arms injured?'

'Not substantially. Why do you ask?'

'I wondered whether he had attempted to ward off the blows with his arms, but that seems not to have been the case, or he would certainly have at least severe bruising, perhaps even a broken arm or two.'

'That's true,' murmured the surgeon, as if the idea was just beginning to form in his mind that I might not be a complete imbecile.

I did not want to look feverishly for the letter and thereby draw attention to it. Apart from any other consideration it was possible that the hospital might argue that it was Velders' property and I had no right to it, even though I was named in it, so as casually as possible I began to go through the clothing, starting with the items least likely to contain a letter.

I will not enumerate the contents of the captain's clothing, observing merely that he was, after all, a sailor, with all that this entails. I must bear in mind that a man might read this book aloud to his womenfolk or servants, who might well be as shocked as I was. The salient point for my purpose was that there was absolutely no sign of the letter, which caused my hands to break out in a sweat.

The logic that was imposing itself upon me was that Velders had clearly stolen the letter believing it to be the Duke of Monmouth's battle plans; and perhaps he had so described it to someone else, maybe at the point of trying to sell it. The villain having paid good money for it then opened and read it, realised that it had been misrepresented, and attacked Velders to recover his money. I suppose one might argue that having demanded a refund he was ethically bound to return the letter, which he had failed to do, but I suppose that is an academic nicety.

Since Velders had a certain amount of money about him when he was attacked, I could only suppose that the attacker had recovered a purse, because it seemed rather cold-blooded to take back loose coins and leave Velders' own money intact. Surely the simple thing to do was to take it all? And if the beating were designed to teach Velders a lesson, would it not have been reinforced by taking all his cash?

The reader may be sure that my brain was working at abnormal speed at this point, and therefore, I fear, somewhat erratically, but I felt very keenly that there was a further complication for me here.

Whoever tried to buy the letter knew now, if he did not before, that there was such a letter. He may well have realised where Velders must have obtained it, since it would not take much to find a Dutch ship newly arrived in the port of London; and it would not take much more to work out that the likeliest person to have the letter was the Stadhouder's emissary, so if he was determined to possess it he knew now where to look for it. Given what he had done to Velders, I could not bear to think what he might do to me. Actually, that is untrue; I found myself increasingly thinking about what he might do to me, and could not help but feel that it would be a good idea to return at once to the ship and persuade Hendriks to put out from the shore a little. About fifty miles would be a good start, I thought.

'You look pale, Master,' the surgeon remarked. 'Are you quite well?'

'Yes,' I replied. It came out as something of a mouse's squeak due to the tension in my throat and the strong emotion that had seized me, namely, fear. I do not believe that I am a coward; I will stand my ground in an argument, however robust, as well as any other man. I just don't like rough stuff; and if a man with a sword can finish up like poor Velders, I hesitated to think what might happen to a philosophy lecturer armed only with a small bible and a pair of velvet gloves .

My thoughts were turned so far inward that I was unaware of the conversation passing between Van Citters and the surgeon. I heard some noise but I was as if in a stupor. It all washed over me. The sense of danger and defeat was overwhelming and I did not know what to do next. I must, of course, do my duty and lose that wretched letter in Exeter somehow, even at the risk of my life. After all, death would be unwelcome, but it might be preferable to going back to The Hague and admitting to William that I had not carried out his orders.

I gnawed at my knuckles in deep thought, and then I saw it. Velders' hat was at the bottom of the pile, and I had done no more than satisfying myself that no letter was concealed in it, which was how I had overlooked the small sprig of herb in his hatband.

CHAPTER TEN

I urgently demanded an answer to a question but nobody seemed to want to give it to me.

'Master, it might help if you asked in English,' Van Citters said quietly.

It was the excitement. My brain could not cope with thinking and speaking English at the same time. I had noticed on my last visit that a number of the young bravoes at the Court of King Charles seemed to have the same problem, and since they had only one language they had given up thinking.

'This herb...' I began.

'It is surely a heather of some kind,' the surgeon announced. 'It is to be found widely in our countryside.'

'I'm sure it is,' I said, 'but I was given some not long since by a gipsy woman in a church nearby.' I showed them my hat with its small floral decoration in the band.

'You think Velders must have met the same woman?' asked Van Citters. He was clearly excited too, because he asked me in Dutch.

'Yes! And if we can find her and she can tell us when and where she met him it may help us to understand how he met his fate.'

'Which church were you in?' demanded the ambassador.

'I have no idea,' I admitted. 'I just climbed the slope from the ship's mooring and headed for the first church I saw.'

'On a slope?' asked Madeley. 'Then you must have been at St Mary-at-Hill.'

'But if the Master was coming towards the ambassador's house he would surely have gone past St Magnus-the-Martyr or St Stephen Walbrook?' the surgeon responded.

'There is only way to settle this,' the ambassador decided. 'Master, you must retrace your steps.'

The little man in the dark blue coat stepped forward. I had forgotten that he was still there. 'It will soon be dusk, gentlemen. If the ambassador permits, we should take his carriage to your ship, Master, and then walk as you walked. Once we find the church, I will ask my fellow watchmen to look for the woman in the district nearby.'

This seemed a sensible plan, and while I might have felt that the watchman was forward in intruding himself into our affairs, there was no denying that the assistance of a number of local men would be very useful.

I asked if we might take Velders' hat, my thinking being that while the woman might not remember Velders, she would probably recognise his navy blue hat with its tawny feather. It was as well that I did.

However, I overlooked one important point, and sat rather shamefaced as the watchman suggested that we should make it our business to detour to the street where Velders had been found, a small lane not far from St Paul's, a famous building site in the middle of the city.

If I may digress briefly, the old St Paul's had been destroyed in a great fire nearly twenty years before, and the alert reader may recall that when I was last in London in 1676 the rebuilding was under way. I was a young man then, yet here I am in my eighties and the new cathedral was only completed within the last ten years — and even now they continue to tinker with it. I can only think that it was constructed by trained snails. [Marginal note: Van der Meer has hastened to explain to me that snails would be poor builders, having no arms to lift things. He takes me altogether too seriously sometimes. Either that, or he thinks my wits are addled.]

We paused briefly in Distaff Lane where we alighted to inspect the place where Velders had been found. He was lying in a narrow passageway on the east side of the street, but the presence of blood in the roadway a few paces to the north made it seem likely that he had been attacked there and dragged into the alley while his person was searched for the stolen letter.

I was perturbed by one feature of this. 'It is late afternoon,' I said, 'and yet there are plenty of people about, and the road at the top of the street seems to be a busy one. Did nobody see Velders being attacked?'

The watchman spread his arms in an expressive gesture. 'We judged the most important matter to be to preserve his life, if God so willed it, Master, so we attended to him first and only returned at about three o'clock to make enquiries.'

'When was he found?'

'Near to midday, I believe.'

'So the assailant had three hours to escape?'

'If not more, for he was not discovered until some time after the attack, I fear. A man who was collecting the work of his piece-workers noted the blood on the road and followed it, raising the cry when he found the captain.'

'And what, pray, do they make in Distaff Lane?' I asked.

'Why, Master, distaffs,' said the watchman, and then said no more upon the subject, so that I was none the wiser. I did not choose to appear obtuse, and so I dropped the matter.

We returned to the carriage and rolled eastwards to the place where the ship was docked.

I know that a great many churches were destroyed in the fire, and yet London has a bewildering number of them. A man might have half a dozen within a short walk of his home, some grander than others, no doubt, but ensuring that anyone must surely find a place to his liking given the wide choice available. These are, of course, wasted on the English, who are largely an irreligious people who delight in telling one the reason why they do not attend this church or that; this one smacks of Popery, while that one lacks good music; the curate at such and such a church preaches too long, while at some other the locals scowl at you whichever seat you occupy.

It suddenly struck me what a heavy responsibility lay upon the shoulders of my friend Compton who was the bishop responsible for all these, leading me to conclude, belatedly, that the episcopal life is not all cakes and ale. The Dutch Reformed Church has no bishops, so the only one I know much about is he to whom I owe obedience as a Catholic priest, the Bishop of Namur, though the particular bishop who had ordained me had long since passed to his reward. In my mind, bishops lived lives of luxury and indolence, spending much of their time fawning on great men and counting their considerable income, but perhaps I was wrong about that.

I was shaken out of this line of thought when the carriage stopped and the others stepped out. I followed suit, and saw that we were above the quayside where the *Nieuwpoort* was berthed.

'Now, Master,' said Van Citters, 'please lead the way.'

I blinked a few times. My immediate reaction was that I had never been here in my life, but that must be nonsense because the *Nieuwpoort* was just behind me. However, places look so different as the sun moves around the sky. The first part of my journey was straightforward. If I was not about to walk on the water, there was only one direction that I could go, up a bank in a northerly direction.

There was a stall to my right that I recollected because it was laden with eels. I had passed that on the previous morning, and I recalled standing for a few moments while I gathered my bearings. I could see a church to my right but I had decided not to enter that one, but to walk towards the ambassador's house first, so I had turned left there.

Another three spires were visible, as was a dome. It was at this point that I realised that I was confusing two separate events; the first day, when I had stepped in the manure and gone to a Catholic church, and that morning, when I had found some other church; and it was then that I remembered turning towards St Paul's.

I had kept to the south side of St Paul's, so I followed that path, the ambassador and the watchman following behind in his carriage, which led me to wonder why I could not have retraced my route from the comfort of that conveyance. I was having a quiet grumble to myself about that injustice when I saw a spire in the distance that looked familiar. I suppose one spire is much the same as another, but this church had a curious shape beneath with decorative gables that might almost have been Dutch.

'What is that church?' I enquired.

The watchman stepped out to follow my pointing arm. 'That is St Martin's-within-Ludgate,' he replied.

'Then St Martin's-within-Ludgate is where I met the gipsy woman.'

'If she was here today she probably wasn't here yesterday, but at least we know she is likely to be somewhere within walking distance,' the watchman explained.

This intelligence was less useful than he seemed to think, given that most of us can walk more than twenty miles in a day if the road is in sound condition.

'She could be anywhere,' I groaned.

'Not at all, Master,' the watchman retorted. 'These gipsies gather in groups and they keep to particular places. They might be in the fields at Islington, or beyond Tyburn. I'll ask my colleagues where they have seen these people congregating.'

'But if there are many of them, how will we know we have the right woman?' I asked.

'I had hoped, Master, that you would be available to identify her.'

There was nothing else for it. It meant more delay before I could depart for Exeter, throw away that confounded letter and return to my homeland which, at that moment, was sweeter than ever to me, but I shrugged, climbed back into the carriage, and allowed myself to be taken back to the *Nieuwpoort*.

CHAPTER ELEVEN

I slept fitfully, tormented by dreams in which I crept up behind Velders and struck him forcefully over the head with my letter. There are those who will tell you that dreams convey truths that are otherwise lost to us, and that analysis of a person's dreams and nightmares may enable us to reconstruct events. If that is so then the truth is a very strange and labile thing, since I have recently dreamed that I have swum across the Rijn only to emerge on the far bank to the realisation that I am naked, that my clothes are neatly folded where I set out, and that the entire population of a great city are looking at me; that I have been elected Pope (in which event you may reasonably suppose that there would be some changes made in the way the Church is run); and that my grandmother has come to ask me yet again why I am still not married, despite the fact that she has been dead since 1679.

My temper was not improved by my forgetting that I was in a ship's cabin and banging my head on a beam when I sat up abruptly during the night. I did not realise until the morning that I had gashed my scalp which bled to such a degree that my bed looked as if I had been attacked. When I appeared at breakfast Wilkens was concerned that I might require the services of a surgeon.

'It's quite a deep cut, Master. Perhaps it should be cauterized or sewn up. Doesn't it hurt?'

'It throbs rather than paining me, but the intermittent bleeding is troublesome.'

'You should see a surgeon, Master.'

'Maybe I will. Could you send the ship's surgeon to me?'

Wilkens looked uncomfortable. 'We don't really have one.'

'Don't have one? Isn't this a naval vessel?'

'Certainly, Master, but we weren't expecting to need a surgeon, and real surgeons are expensive, so we only have a barber.'

Judging by the state of the sailors' hair, he was not much of a barber either.

'When I say barber,' Wilkens continued miserably, 'I mean he used to work as an assistant to a barber. But I will send for him.'

A few minutes later the door opened and the malodorous individual who had grinned at me when I fell asleep on watch was ushered into the cabin.

'What you done then?' he asked cheerily.

I ducked my head to allow him to see the damage.

'Oh, that's nothing. A bit of a clean-up and some salt and you'll soon be as handsome as ever!' he declared with appalling jocularity, pushing me down into a chair and opening a canvas roll in which he had a range of unpleasant and none too clean instruments. To me they looked more like a torturer's tools, but he selected one with care, asked for a cup of wine and bent my neck towards the light.

I found myself hoping he did not intend to drink the wine first, but he took up a napkin from the breakfast table, dipped it in the wine and began dabbing at my scalp.

'Quite deep,' he murmured. 'You have a soft head, Master. We sailors do this most days without mishap.'

'Mine hasn't been toughened by years of banging it against beams,' I admitted.

'Too much book learning,' he suggested. 'It makes your brains flabby.'

I would have resented such a remark from anyone, but from a scrofulous and impudent sailor it was almost insupportable. However, I judged that annoying him while he was doing me a service was not a prudent move, and instead resolved to mention his name to the Stadhouder when my mission was completed, desiring him to discharge the wretch and thus to gain my belated revenge for such familiarity.

'Have you any genever?' he asked, which Wilkens passed to him, not without a measure of concern.

I felt my head burn as the spirit was dribbled along the cut.

'Smarts a bit, do it?' the villain smirked. 'That'll be the fight twixt the spirit and the poison in the wound. Besides, there's a fair splinter of wood sticking into your head there, but if I just get my trusty tweezers I can...' Whatever he was going to say was drowned out by my cry of pain as he yanked what felt like a small tree from my bruised crown. 'There we has it!' the blackguard cried, and showed it to me. 'You're lucky I was around, or that might have worked its way into your brains and caused all manner of mischief.'

This seemed to be a prediction in defiance of all known anatomy. Surely the point of a skull was to stop splinters entering the brain?

Through gritted teeth I thanked him as he rolled up his tools once more and left his empty hand dangling for a few seconds until it dawned on me that he was hoping for some concrete expression of gratitude from me.

'Away with you now!' Wilkens interrupted. 'That's what you're paid for.'

When we were alone I made my first move towards retaliation. 'What is that man's name?' I asked.

Wilkens looked at the closed door as if that might help his recollection. 'Him? I don't know, Master. He only joined the ship the day we sailed. But then, so did a lot of others. The Stadhouder doesn't like paying men between voyages so he prefers to sign them off and sign them back on again. It only saves a small amount per man but when you have eighty of them, it all adds up.'

That sounded like the Stadhouder's mode of thought. I mused, not for the first time, on the likelihood that if I were killed on one of these missions William would regard it as slightly unfortunate but console himself that he would save my fee. Not that any fee had been promised, you understand. I thought it probable that the money he gave me after my last trip to London was only offered because King Charles II had already given me some, and William did not want to appear parsimonious.

I was still at my breakfast when someone arrived to tell me that the ambassador was waiting for me, so I hurriedly swallowed some bread and half a cup of ale and ran to join him. I still had my cap in my hand which allowed him to recoil in horror at the sight of my scalp.

[Marginal note: for the benefit of Van der Meer and other such scurrilous spreaders of calumny, my hair was not then thin on top. I will allow that in my later years it has lost its luxuriant thickness, but the only reason that he could see my scalp was that the would-be barber had soaked my head in genever.]

'Master Mercurius! What has befallen you?' he asked.

I explained the sequence of events that I have set out.

'Thank goodness for that! I feared that you had been attacked like poor Velders.'

I doubted that Velders had banged his head on the beam above his bed, but then I realised why the ambassador might have thought that and went a little pale. If anyone wanted to cave my skull in I had already given them a bit of a helping hand myself.

I climbed into the carriage as invited, and together we returned to St Martin's-within-Ludgate, where the watchman was waiting for us.

'By your leave, gentlemen, I'll join you and we'll go to the place where the woman has been found, near the Temple Church.' He smiled thinly. 'I'm surprised she was so close to Bridewell. It may save us a lot of trouble.'

I did not understand his reference, which must have shown in my face because the ambassador explained it to me.

'Bridewell is an old palace, part of which is now a prison,' he explained.

I was alarmed to think that this officer was considering locking up this poor woman for no good reason other than having been near to the site of an attack. It had never crossed my mind that she might be the perpetrator of it. For one thing, she was too short to have hit Velders on the top of the head, and although he may not have anticipated danger I think that if he saw an old woman placing a step-stool behind him he might have been on his guard.

She might, I allowed, be an accomplice. Suppose that she worked with a man. She engages a likely victim in conversation, persuades him to buy a sprig of heather, offers to place it in his hatband and, when he removes his hat so that she may do so, her assistant batters in his defenceless skull and makes off with his valuables.

There were some difficulties with this conjecture. First, Velders' valuables were still in his clothes, so far as we knew. Second, given the force of the assault, removing a soft hat would appear to be somewhat unnecessary. Third, I had removed my hat and not been clobbered. I can accept that I am not as obviously wealthy as a naval captain, but then why bother with me at all? I guessed that I had been approached because one who prays might be more likely to give alms to the needy. Had Velders been praying?

We had arrived at the Temple Church, so that matter would have to wait for a while. We were ushered inside and found two guards standing beside a chair in which the elderly Romany woman was sitting, though she jumped to her feet as we entered and bobbed briefly but respectfully. She looked terrified.

When she saw me, her hand flew to her mouth as if to stifle some inappropriate remark. Did she think that I was her accuser? Or was I the avenging angel who could see into the darkness of her deeds, or that of her accomplice?

She gripped, still, the little basket of herbs, her knuckles moving as she fidgeted with the handle. She seemed even smaller than I had remembered, but then I had not really looked at her. It is strange that we do not look at the poor, even as we hand them some alms, as if their eyes will contain some reproach rather than gratitude; as if they are thinking "You who have so much, you could do more for me"; as if they know that we have not learned a proper sense of gratitude that we are not like them.

'Is this the woman?' asked the watchman.

'It is,' I replied.

He lifted the woman's chin. 'Do you remember giving this gentleman a sprig of heather for his hat?'

'I didn't give it. He bought it, honest and legal,' she replied.

'And do you remember where this was?'

She shrugged. 'Some big church nearby. He was a-praying and talking to himself. What does he say I done, because I never did! I'm a decent Romany woman.'

'Now calm yourself! Nobody thinks you've done anything wrong, but you may be able to help these gentlemen.'

Her tongue flicked over her lips like a lizard's as she attempted to assess what her help might be worth. Threepence? Sixpence, if she could satisfy us sufficiently.

The watchman spoke lower. I do not think I was meant to hear his words. 'The religious gent has some questions. Answer him true. And speak slowly and clearly, for they're foreign gentlemen, and not used to English.'

This may have been true of me, but it was markedly unfair on the ambassador.

'Madam,' I said, 'the day before you did this service for me, I believe you did the same to a countryman of ours. This is his hat, in which you may see the little plant in the band. Do you know the hat?'

She took it and turned it to the light. 'Another foreign gentleman? Broader than you, and with a sword.'

'Yes! Shortly afterwards he was attacked and now lies between life and death at a hospital. Can you recall when and where you met him?'

She nibbled at her nails in thought. ''Twas in the forenoon.'

'What hour of the clock?'

'After ten o'clock, I think.'

'And where did you meet him?'

She gnawed at her thumb once more. 'I don't rightly recall. It wasn't far from here.'

If only I knew London better. I had gone with Velders to the ambassador's house, then we had walked back together until we had separated, but I had been so distressed by the state of my boots that I had paid no attention to my surroundings.

Suddenly a notion came to me. 'I rinsed my boots at a public pump! The pump was at the side of the road. Velders was with me then. That's where we separated.'

The watchman looked at the two guards.

'Might be at the Haymarket,' suggested one.

'Surely Pump Court?' the other responded.

'Pump Court is close at hand,' agreed the watchman, 'but you heard the gentleman say that the pump was by the side of the road, and the pump in Pump Court stands in the middle. And surely the Haymarket is above a mile away?'

'But if no-one charged the gentleman for the water, where else could it be?' the guard persisted.

'Charged?' I stuttered.

'Water in this city being in short supply,' Van Citters explained, 'there is money to be made in bringing it here. Householders pay for their supply and the companies charge for use of standpipes or pumps. If nobody charged you, the likely reason is that they saw you were a clergyman, and if you are a clergyman the supply must have been...'

'A church supply!' the watchman interrupted. 'St Paul's.'

'But I know the cathedral,' I said. 'I would have recognised that.'

'Indeed you would, sir,' agreed the watchman, 'but there is a pump to the rear that once served the houses behind and was refurbished after the fire to provide water for the builders.'

There was some more conversation that immediately followed this, but I cannot record it for I was too busy trying to come to the terms with the idea of paying for water. When you come from a land where we live our lives with water on all sides, the notion that someone might charge you to help yourself to it takes some getting used to; even if a Dutchman wanted to charge for it — and we are sufficiently commercially-minded to do so — the practicalities of stopping someone taking it at will militate against any charge. Having said that, I would not drink any Leiden water that had not been skimmed, sieved and boiled first. The woolworkers discard their washings into the canals and there is often a noisome layer of grease from the fleece floating on the surface. If you have ever smelled a wet sheep you will know what I mean. All in all, the safest course was to convert the water into good ale, where the boiling and malting render it safe and palatable, and the finings clear the more offensive material. Even small children in Leiden drink ale. Infant mortality is high enough without the extra hazard of giving them water.

When I recovered myself the watchman and Van Citters were discussing how well this information fitted with what we already knew.

'Well, Master,' the ambassador pronounced, 'this is very gratifying. I am informed that from the pump at the rear of St Paul's a man might look towards the river and see it as he looked down Distaff Lane.'

This made sense to me. How does a naval man navigate in any city that he does not know well? Surely he makes for the nearest part of the river and follows it back to his ship. If Velders had been doing that it would explain why he was in Distaff Lane, and the timings could be made to work quite well too, given that they were rather imprecise. Velders must have been attacked at the earliest opportunity after he left me. If that were so, it raised a very uncomfortable thought in my mind. Someone must have been watching us.

I knew a blind woman once and asked her what she found most difficult about her condition. To my surprise, it was not being unable to read, or having to cook by touch. She said it was never knowing whether you are being watched. Her senses were heightened so that she could hear the breathing of anyone in the room, but she never knew if there was someone outside the window spying on her. Until that moment I suppose that I had never really understood what she meant; but I had been completely unaware of anyone spying on us on the morning that Velders was attacked, and if I had not detected a voyeur then, why should I suppose that I was not being watched now?

I willingly accepted the ambassador's invitation to dine with him, if only because I did not like the idea of walking the streets of London on my own, but all through the meal my mind was turning over these troubling matters.

'What will you do now, Master?' Van Citters asked, pushing a platter of cheese towards me and offering me the basket of bread.

'I do not know, Ambassador.'

There are a great many things that I do not know. Some of them do not trouble me at all, such as the name of the Emperor of China. Some are not vexing, but there is a certain natural curiosity involved that leads me to think it would be good to know them if I could find the answer without much effort; I would love to understand brewing, for example, or why we ride horses but not cows. I can watch people weaving for hours without ever quite being able to comprehend how they produce the finished cloth. Unfortunately the puzzle of Velders' assailant was not in this category.

'I feel uneasy that I do not understand what has occurred here,' I explained. 'As you know, I have a letter that I must deliver.'

'Or lose,' Van Citters interjected helpfully.

'Indeed. I believe that Velders thought he had stolen that, when actually he had taken my letter of accreditation as an emissary of the Stadhouder. When we docked he accompanied me ashore to come here, then he said he must provision his ship and we parted.'

'He said what?' said Van Citters, sitting up abruptly with unusual energy.

'He said he must provision his ship.'

'Why, in God's name?' Van Citters reddened a little. 'I beg your pardon. A poor choice of words before a clergyman. But no captain needs to reprovision on a round trip from Hellevoetsluis to London. He will be fully stocked upon leaving and apart from a barrel of drinking water, he should not need to buy more here, especially at London prices.'

This last comment rang very true with me. The Stadhouder would certainly not pay in England for something he could wheedle out of his subjects at a reduced cost.

'I must concede,' I allowed, 'that I was deceived on that point. But what, then, did he go to do? Let us suppose that he has my letter — or thinks he has — and wants to use it to his profit. He might take it to the King, but I cannot imagine that King James would give any credit to a letter delivered by a Dutchman.'

'Via a courtier, then?'

'But who would Velders know? He would have to trust the recipient to deliver it into the King's hands, but then he would have to know someone here, and so far as I know he did not. I know more people here than he did.'

'Well, then,' said Van Citters, 'to whom would you take it?'

I thought a while. 'Arlington is out of favour. I would trust the Bishop of London but he is not in favour at Court, being a staunch opponent of Catholicism.' I racked my brains. There must be someone I had met before who was still alive. 'Mr

Pepys!' I exclaimed at last. 'He saved my life when I was last here. If he still lives I would trust him completely.'

'A man with plenty of business in the docks,' Van Citters observed. 'He is Secretary to the Admiralty for the King. If he received your letter and presented it to the King, it would be credited, I have no doubt, so long as Pepys himself was convinced. Maybe you should give it to him?'

It was a tempting idea but I had been told to lose it in the West Country, not to give it to one of the King's Secretaries, and if Pepys suspected that he was being used as part of a deception I would lose a friend and the plot would fail. But might Velders have known Pepys too? There was only one way to resolve that question. I must ask him.

CHAPTER TWELVE

Van Citters could not spare his carriage, he being engaged to attend upon the King that evening, but he summoned a couple of young men with stout sticks to accompany me around London and see that I came to no harm. To be perfectly honest, I was more afraid of them than I was of any others. They spoke in some local argot of which I could discern little and exchanged ribald and coarse comments as we walked along, of which I understood only too much. After a pretty maid passed us and they made several remarks about her person of a most unfitting nature I felt obliged to remonstrate with them.

'Perhaps, gentlemen, when you say such things you will reflect that I am a minister of religion?' I growled.

'Sorry,' said one. 'We didn't know you wanted to say something first.'

'No,' agreed the other, 'we didn't fink you'd be interested in the size of a girl's…'

'I'm not!' I quickly assured them. 'But if people believe that you are my servants they will expect me to have trained you to behave with more decorum.'

'Decorum?'

'Respect, then. More decently.'

'Oh, right. Sorry, Master.'

We walked on, and no more approving remarks were made about young women, though one of them pointed to a matron bending over and mimed throwing a saddle over her until he saw my deep frown.

Mr Pepys was at home, and welcomed me cordially, offering me glasses of several intoxicating cordials and pressing me to stay to supper, which I could not.

'It has been such a long time, Master,' he said.

'It has, Mr Pepys.'

'Samuel, I beg. No ceremony. And what brings you here?'

I judged it best not to reveal the whole story, so I resolved to make no mention of that confounded letter, despite the fact that the genuine one was tight against my breast as we spoke. 'It is a matter of some delicacy,' I said. 'May I speak frankly and in confidence?'

'Of course. Mum's the word.'

'I do not understand. Why is your mother involved?'

Pepys shook his head. 'It means that I will be silent. Like a mummer. You know, a player upon the stage.'

If English actors do not speak, their playhouses must be very strange places, I thought, but said nothing. 'Well then, I am here upon a mission for the Stadhouder. You may be aware that the Duke of Monmouth is presently in my country.'

'It is the talk of London,' Pepys replied. 'We wonder what your master's intentions are.'

'I can set your mind at rest,' I replied. 'I am here to encourage those who have my master's interests at heart not to support the Duke's plans. The Stadhouder hopes in this way to avoid bloodshed by demonstrating to the Duke the futility of any attempt at an invasion.'

'I am pleased to hear it,' said Pepys, 'but frankly that is what the Stadhouder would say if he were poised to send thirty thousand soldiers among us.'

He doesn't have thirty thousand soldiers, I wanted to say, because he won't pay for them, but that seemed to be an inappropriate thing for an envoy to remark. 'I am sure,' I said guardedly, 'that His Majesty will be aware from his own sources that no such army is congregating in the United Provinces.'

Pepys laughed. 'And I am sure that you are right.'

He refilled my glass. There was a serious risk that I would forget my mission and, indeed, my name if this level of hospitality endured much longer.

I need hardly say that Pepys was deceived, because the English Ambassador to The Hague was, as we noted earlier, a dolt, but it suited my purposes to let him go on believing that no invasion plan was being made.

'I have reason to believe,' I continued, 'that the master of the ship that brought me here, Captain Velders, may have had some previous connection with someone here. It is likely that Velders intended to undermine the Stadhouder's plan by spreading the falsehood that a large army was being recruited. I believe that he met someone as soon as we arrived and that this contact, or someone who was an onlooker, attacked Velders so that he now lies between life and death in St Bartholomew's hospital.'

Pepys was often accused of being a hedonist and shallow thinker, but he quickly grasped the importance of my words. 'Is Velders being guarded?'

'No. I have no men...'

'He should be,' Pepys interrupted. 'If someone thought he needed killing before and failed to do so, a further attempt is likely. Excuse me while I make the necessary arrangements. Help yourself to port wine.'

I poured a dribble into my glass to give the impression that I had taken a full glass and drained it down. My brain must have been addled by all this drink, because I had completely overlooked the possibility that the assassin would attempt to complete his task.

Pepys returned and poured himself another glass which he sipped with every sign of enjoyment.

'I am surprised,' Pepys remarked after a moment, 'that the watch did not think to inform my office that a foreign sea captain had been attacked here.'

'You would expect to hear such a thing?'

'Certainly. We do not want overseas wars conducted on our soil, Master.'

I must have looked uncommonly puzzled because Pepys developed his thought for me.

'Let us suppose that, for example, there is some enmity betwixt France and Spain. It would not be surprising if French and Spanish ships were berthed here and their sailors mingled at some dockside tavern. It cannot have a happy outcome, Master. Quite apart from the damage done by a brawl, we do not want to give either country cause to accuse us of not protecting their citizens. For that reason we keep in close contact with the constables.' He smiled thinly. 'We noted, for example, the arrival of the *Nieuwpoort*, though I confess that I did not anticipate that among her passengers would be an old friend.'

He saluted me with his glass, which salute I returned.

'I think, Samuel, that it was not realised that he was a sea captain, though the Ambassador was notified that he appeared to be Dutch upon inspection of some papers upon his person.'

Pepys frowned. 'Perhaps so. Nevertheless, prudence dictates that the matter ought to have been referred to others better placed to assess the position.'

By which I took it he meant himself. The life of underlings must be a very difficult one, I thought; if they refer too much they are thought fussy and lacking in initiative, whereas if they refer too little they are chastised for slackness in their duties. As one who spent much of his life as an underling I am only too aware that pleasing one's masters is never as straightforward as they would have you believe. William, for example, while admirably lacking in vindictiveness, had a very simple test for determining the right course of action for his servants to take; whatever was right for William must, ipso facto, be right for the country. The trick was to spot when he was about to change his mind. Bouwman, his private secretary, was exceptionally good at this. Whenever William gave verbal orders and instructed Bouwman to set them forth in a letter, he was unfailingly satisfied with Bouwman's effort. I was intrigued to know how this was possible, until Bouwman confessed that he often prepared two entirely different documents and only produced the one that better suited William's second thoughts.

'Forgive me, Samuel,' I said tentatively, 'but I must ask. Is it possible that Velders was meeting one of your agents?'

I feared that Pepys might be offended by the question, but he received it calmly and gave it some moments' consideration before replying.

'I think not. Until she arrived we did not know that the *Nieuwpoort* was coming. You will know better than me when her master received his orders, but I cannot imagine that it was planned long enough in advance for us to have heard that she was to voyage here. In any event, I cannot conceive how Captain Velders could have communicated anything in advance, since his ship is surely faster than any other means of sending the message. Perhaps one day, Master, ingenious men will devise a means of transmitting a message through the air, but until they do, a ship such as the *Nieuwpoort* must be the quickest bearer of tidings.'

It was my turn to frown. Velders may have known that he was coming to England, but he did not know why until that moment in the inn when William informed him. Pepys was quite right. There had been no time to send a message in advance of his arrival, neither could he have done so when we docked without my knowledge, for we walked together from the ship into the city.

My head was starting to hurt. Of course, I blamed Pepys' port wine, but accepted another glass.

CHAPTER THIRTEEN

The two Londoners appointed by Van Citters must have seen me safely back to the ship, though I woke on the following morning feeling as if I had been repeatedly coshed. I have little head for wine, and I am unused to port wine in particular. The English drink large amounts of it and consequently a great many Englishmen suffer from the gout and are to be seen sitting in assembly rooms with a bandaged foot resting on a cushion. I may mention in passing that they are excused from dancing at such entertainments, which seems to me to be an adequate cause to adopt the stratagem of pretending to have the gout so as to be spared the embarrassment of demonstrating my inability to move my own feet to music in the correct way.

On this particular morning I think I can safely say that the only part of me that was not aching was my feet. I must have climbed into my bunk in a very tired state and had somehow trapped one arm beneath my body, so that it was temporarily useless but throbbed as the life came back into it; my head had been hard up against the cabin wall so that I had a crick in my neck and in attempting to rectify my position on waking I banged my head on a beam once more and struck my knee forcefully on the bed frame. I therefore appeared for breakfast with my head tipped to one side, one arm vigorously rubbing the other, and hobbling due to a sore knee. On top of that, my mouth felt as if someone had woven a tapestry around my tongue and every movement of my jaw sent darts of pain through my teeth and cheekbones.

'Heavy night, Master?' smiled Hendriks.

'Not at all,' I replied with as much dignity as I could summon. 'I am not finding it easy to sleep on a ship, that's all.'

'You snored lustily,' Hendriks said, as if tempting me to deny that I had been in my cups.

'I apologise if I disturbed you,' I said. 'It is a measure of my discomfort if I snored, for I never do so at home.'

Actually, I do not know whether that is true or not, because I do not sleep in company with others. [Marginal note: Van der Meer began to say something but bit his tongue. I believe that the blackguard intended to accuse me of snoring while napping in my chair. Of course, this is untrue, because I do not nod off while dictating to him. Who knows what drivel he would write if I did?]

I took a beaker of small beer and some bread. I had thought to take some cheese too, but as I approached the platter the smell of the cheese persuaded me that this would be a very bad idea. I may add that even while berthed a ship rocks gently on the water, and at that moment it felt as if it were riding six foot waves.

'Master,' Hendriks began as I took my place at the table, 'I should be glad of your advice. The authorities here wish us to vacate the berth to allow another ship to dock. I can, of course, lay up in the river and we can go back and forth in the ship's boat, but if you mean only to be here another day or so I could ask them for leave to remain here. There will be a fee, of course.'

Mention of a fee did not surprise me. King Charles had invented all manner of taxes and charges and his brother was simply following his precedent. If the English could charge for drinking water then I was sure that they could charge a ship for staying still. I was fairly sure too that if they could think of a way of charging foreigners for breathing English air they would do it — though I was equally certain that William was no slouch when it came to taxing his subjects and could be just as inventive.

It troubled me that we could even think of leaving without solving the mystery of who had attacked Velders, but I was making no progress with that enquiry and I needed to lose that wretched letter before the Duke of Monmouth upset the apple-cart by arriving in England with the army I had denied to Pepys that he had, and whose projected movements were detailed in a document currently inside my undershirt. I had a momentary shock as I realised that I had not checked that the letter was still there, but as I moved my arm I felt the document scrape across my chest in a reassuring way.

'Lieutenant,' I said, 'I think we must set sail for Exeter later today. It may be necessary to return here after my mission there is complete so that we can collect Captain Velders and return him to his homeland and his family.'

'Of course,' Hendriks replied. 'That is only fitting. If you will excuse me, I will give the necessary orders.'

He rose from the table with a polite bow, and left me to consider how much bread would remain in my stomach if I once managed to swallow it; but I gave up the effort, and settled for a breakfast of small beer.

It was necessary to keep the ambassador apprised of my movements so after breakfast I walked into town once more. Since the two swaggering youths the ambassador had provided were no longer there I asked Hendriks if I might be accompanied by a couple of his sailors to ensure my safety against possible attack, and in a few minutes I was walking through the streets flanked by a pair of men. One was that so-called barber-surgeon, while the other was one of the ship's carpenters.

'I hope you've got a good sound pair of boots,' the barber-surgeon said, 'for the streets are full of filth.'

'I reckon we were picked because we both have shoes,' the carpenter added. 'This is no place for a man with bare feet.'

'Nor without a hat,' his colleague agreed. 'I've seen three chamber pots emptied from the windows already and we've barely gone two hundred paces.'

I had been too busy watching my feet to notice this, and had naively assumed that it had started to rain. The thought of what might be running down my back was quite off-putting.

We Dutch are much more sanitary than the English. As you walk the streets of London there are Englishmen — and even women — in doorways and alleyways attending to the calls of nature. In a few places there are screens or huts to provide some privacy, but they are not numerous. Most Dutch women would not condescend to such a practice, if only because the floor would not be clean enough.

The ambassador was out when we arrived, so I wrote a note thanking him for his hospitality and assistance, explaining my movements and undertaking to return if I could to resume the quest for Velders' attacker. I pondered whether I should tell him the whole truth about the Duke of Monmouth's plans, but decided that if William had wanted him to know more than the ambassador already knew then he would have given me a letter for him. It was entirely possible that neither of us would have been able to decipher his handwriting, but at least I would have known that such a letter existed.

As we left I could not help but notice my companions chomping on a pastry while the barber-surgeon was polishing an apple on his malodorous breeches.

'Nice girl, that maid was,' he said with a horrible leer. 'Shame we couldn't stay a day or two more. I reckon we'd have got a lot more than an apple off her.'

I know that sailors are not renowned for their delicacy of feeling, but I seemed to have been saddled with a particularly unsavoury lot. 'Aren't you married men?' I asked sharply.

'I am,' said the carpenter, 'but you'll notice I said nothing about the maid.'

'You may have said nothing,' his colleague announced, 'but I saw the look you gave her backside.'

'Is it too much to hope that you would remember that I am a minister of religion?' I snapped.

'Sorry, Master,' said the carpenter.

'What he said,' agreed the barber-surgeon, the impudent rogue. I could see why ships' officers regularly resorted to the lash. I felt like ordering a flogging for him myself.

I am not well versed in nautical matters, but I understand that when you are sailing down a river you have to take into account both the wind and the tide. I had thought that we would have to wait for the tide to start going out, but Hendriks explained that all we needed was for it to stop coming in, so we departed earlier than I had expected. This was good for two reasons. First, it meant we would not be in the busiest part of the river after darkness fell, and second, the less time we spent in London the better. Of course, I regretted not having been able to pay my respects once more to the Bishop of London, but I had his letter of introduction to his counterpart in Exeter and with luck I expected to be returning towards Hellevoetsluis within the week. I would then rush to The Hague to report to William, humbly accept any small token of gratitude he offered (and it would be small), and return to Leiden with all haste to reclaim my room and have a very large beaker of ale in the inn on the Langebrug.

Wilkens came to stand beside me as I gazed out over the rail, or whatever they call that thing along the side of a ship.

'Are you sorry to be leaving London, Master?'

'Not in the least. I should shake its dust from my feet.'

The young man smiled. 'I have never seen Exeter, Master, but I doubt it is the equal of London.'

'It may not be any better, mijnheer Wilkens, but it cannot be any worse.'

How wrong I was.

CHAPTER FOURTEEN

I am not a man much given to complaining [Marginal note: Van der Meer so far forgot himself as to laugh immoderately at this comment and then tried to excuse himself by claiming that he had hiccups] but that voyage was tedious.

The tide took us out to the mouth of the Thames, where we met with a north wind that took us sweetly beyond Dover. The speed of this part of the journey may have raised my expectations of the rest, for despite some complicated zigzagging manoeuvres we made little headway for some time. This allowed Englishmen to gather on the top of the cliffs and abuse us heartily, apparently for no other reason than that we were Dutch. This abuse was accompanied by gestures of the vilest kind and the frequent displaying of bare buttocks, which seems to pass for wit amongst some classes of Englishmen — and, I regret to say, some Englishwomen.

At length we picked up some wind and began to make our westward way pausing at the Isle of Wight to buy fresh fish from the locals at exorbitant prices and then finding that the winds were again contrary, so that having quitted the Isle in the morning, we were very near back there in the afternoon. I asked Hendriks, only half in jest, if it would be quicker to ride the prevailing wind via the East Indies and the Americas and approach Exeter from the west, but he assured me that we would be in that city within a day or two; inside a week at the very worst (God willing).

That night a storm arose which tossed the ship violently and made me wish I had not partaken of the fish stew. Those fish were duly returned to the sea, albeit somewhat masticated, and when lightning flashed nearby I was so surprised that I rolled off my bunk and struck my head on the chamber pot. I hurriedly riffled through my bible looking for the Gospel passage in which Our Lord calms the stormy Sea of Galilee when the apostles thought that they were like to die, and the reader may be assured that my prayers were every bit as fervent as theirs.

The storm died down, and as daylight came we found ourselves in a pleasant bay. After tidying my appearance I searched for Hendriks, and found him having breakfast.

'Sleep well, Master?' he enquired.

'Barely at all, thank you,' I replied, at which he seemed surprised. 'Did you not notice the tremendous storm?' I continued.

'Storm? That little squall? Well, it's behind us now, Master.'

I am sure that this was mere braggadocio on his part, for no man could have been at peace during that tempest, awake or asleep, but I let it pass to preserve my dignity.

Hendriks was inspecting a chart closely.

'Where are we?' I enquired.

'I'm not exactly sure,' he answered. 'I'll have a better idea at noon, when I can measure our latitude, but somewhere around here seems likely.' He indicated an area of sea with a great sweep of his arm that seemed to encompass half the water between England and France.

'So is that the English or French coast I can see?' I asked.

'The English,' Hendriks announced confidently.

'And you have established that using your instruments?'

'No. The locals on the cliff-top are abusing us in English. If we were on the other side of the water we would be abused in French.'

Let me explain something that I have observed about sailors. They seem to be remarkably unconcerned about not knowing exactly where they are. I cannot imagine, for example, that a general marching his troops across Europe would be comfortable with knowing that they were "probably in Germany" or "somewhere in the Holy Roman Empire, more than likely". Yet the average sailor seems quite content with only really knowing where they are for a few minutes either side of midday, when the sun is overhead and they can do some kind of measurements with one of those brass things; even then, they know their latitude but they have to estimate how far east or west they have travelled. It all seemed a bit haphazard to me.

I realise that the intelligent reader — which, of course, describes the majority of those who pick up my books — may think that I exaggerate my lack of understanding of the sea and ships. I doubt that I could, since the deficiency in my knowledge is considerable. The United Provinces would not be a major maritime power if I were directing its affairs, since I still do not really understand how ships can go in opposite directions driven by the same wind. Nevertheless, somehow, they do; perhaps at different speeds, but they do. One has no such conceptual difficulties with the horse, assuming they condescend to go at all. However, with a horse, I expect to ride it all the way to my destination, so I was surprised in the afternoon when a small boat came alongside while we were still at sea, and an official looking man in a blue coat climbed up a rope ladder without, apparently, any invitation nor surprise at his boldness in doing so.

It turned out that he was a pilot, a man whose job is to steer ships safely into harbour using the local knowledge of shallows and channels that he possesses. It seems that, although we were faced with a very substantial expanse of water before us, parts of it were treacherous, so a local sailor is the best man to steer us in. As to how he knew that his services were needed, it appears that there is some method of indicating with flags that you wish to enter the port. Do not expect me to explain how that is done. I was too busy giving grateful thanks to God that we had by some miracle found the right piece of coastline to notice any such signal.

Having been in London for a little while I had sensed that my English was returning to me. My fluency was improving; so it was a shock to me that when the pilot spoke I understood not one word of what he said. Hendriks, however, did, and the two mumbled incomprehensibly for a few minutes before the pilot assumed control of the ship and Hendriks broke off to explain the matter to me.

'You will see from the pilot's chart, Master, that the port of Exeter is actually some way up the river, and the river is quite a narrow one. The pilot suggests that if time is pressing it may be quicker to dock at a small place called Topsham, which is about an hour's walk from the city, or to transfer there to a small boat and be rowed upstream, for the wind is contrary at present.'

'And how long will it take to row?' I asked.

Hendriks inspected the water. 'With the tide running as it is, perhaps an hour and a half. It may be a little longer than walking, but you would arrive fresher. Or we could take a chance on being able to find a carriage in Topsham. The inn is sure to have one for the procurement of supplies.'

I may not be the most seasoned traveller in the world but an objection occurred to me. 'Wouldn't an inn have a cart rather than a carriage?'

'Possibly,' admitted Hendriks. 'But at least your trunk could go with you.'

'I hope not to be in Exeter long enough to need my trunk,' I replied. 'I'll just put a few important items in a bag, sufficient for a couple of days.'

'As you wish,' Hendriks agreed. 'So, is it to be boat or walk?'

I am not a lecturer of the most renowned university in the United Provinces for nothing, and my keen intellect immediately seized upon the false dichotomy presented here. 'Since I must leave the ship to join the boat anyway, cannot that be done just as well at the quay at Topsham?' I enquired. 'So, we may dock there and make enquiry of a carriage or horse, and, if there be none, I can resort to a boat.'

You could see that this reasoning had escaped Hendriks by the way his eyebrows danced around as he contemplated this logic, but at length he assented and withdrew to convey this proposal to the pilot. The pilot touched his hat in salute and called something to me, though I have no idea what he said, since it appeared to contain no vowels.

We came at last to the quay at Topsham and I was able to disembark. I found an inn where the landlord suggested that I take some refreshment while he made enquiries about a cart. At least, that is what Hendriks told me he said. There was some prolonged discussion between the two of them before the landlord put a tankard of execrable ale in front of each of us and left us alone.

I glanced around me and was surprised at once by a very familiar sight. 'Aren't those Dutch houses?' I asked.

Hendriks followed my gaze. 'In style, certainly. The ships that trade from our land to England collect wool here, but they come empty, or, more accurately, under ballast. They then have to do something with the ballast before they can load the wool.

They came to realise that people here value Dutch bricks, so they often bring bricks here, and sell them to the local builders, who have a fancy to build in the Dutch style.'

'May I ask what the landlord was saying?' I said, since Hendriks seemed to have no plan to tell me unless I demanded an explanation.

'Certainly. It seems that for many years there was rivalry between this town and the city upriver, so the local lord blocked the river to force the commerce to his harbour. It is only in recent years that the blockage has been removed and a canal cut to allow the city's trade to resume. But the landlord says it silts up regularly and he doubts that our ship will easily make the trip, if at all. A boat that draws half a fathom or so is much better suited to it, he says.'

I was exasperated by all this obscuring language. 'What, pray, does that mean in plain Dutch?'

'That the water is only three feet deep in places.'

Put in those terms I could see good reason why the *Nieuwpoort* was not the best option, and my original intention of impressing the locals with the stateliness of my vessel as we docked at the city quay was foolish.

On the other hand, I could see a ship not much smaller than ours coming downriver, so it must have gone upriver in the first place; and the pilot had not refused point-blank to make the attempt, as any sane man would if the trip were impossible. But the clinching argument in my eyes was that William had ordered the *Nieuwpoort* to Exeter, not to Topsham. Well, that was the key public argument that I deployed; the private one was that I wanted that ship near at hand when I had lost that confounded letter so that I could get away and back to sea with all speed.

After all, who wouldn't?

CHAPTER FIFTEEN

The landlord had secured a cart. Never mind that anyone sitting in it would look like a condemned man being transported in ignominy to the scaffold. I do not think that I had seen a cart before with wheels that did not match; by which I mean that while the diameter of each may have been the same, one was slightly thicker and brightly painted.

Hendriks had accepted that his orders, strictly construed, enjoined him to berth the ship at Exeter, but on the advice of the pilot — I had to take his word for this given the incomprehensibility of the man's speech — he proposed to make the attempt on the next rising tide, when the channel would be at its greatest depth, so I might expect the ship to be at the City Quay by the middle of the following day at the latest.

Thus mollified, I took my travelling bag and mounted the cart, asking Hendriks to ensure that the driver knew where we were going. I expressly requested him to take me by way of the City Quay so that I would know where to go to rejoin the *Nieuwpoort*, and held up a shiny coin to reinforce the idea. Curiously, although I could not understand him, he seemed to have no problem in comprehending me, smiled contentedly, displaying a set of teeth like a wrecked graveyard, and chirpily recited 'Bishop's Palace — City Quay!' before accepting the coin and attempting to bite it, at which I was somewhat aggrieved, as if a man of the cloth would pass false coin. However, after a few minutes' reflection I had made a mental list of at least four clerics I knew whose money certainly merited surreptitious testing, including at least one bishop, so I resolved not to be so censorious.

Any attempt at conversation with the driver seemed doomed to frustration, since we appeared not to share a language. I admit that I did not try Latin on him, but in any event he was engaged in talking non-stop to the horse, as if even a moment without exhortation would cause the animal to cease forward progress. I think I caught the horse's name as Jinny, or possibly Jenny. It might even have been Jeremy, except that I looked under its belly on mounting and knew that it did not qualify as a Jeremy.

Surprisingly quickly we could see the cathedral in the distance, which at least gave me some assurance that we were indeed headed for Exeter. I had a small book with me which I read as we plodded along, so the time passed pleasantly enough as we threaded our way into the city.

The small book was actually a notebook in which I had recorded some information given to me by Dr Compton, the Bishop of London, about the Bishop of Exeter, Dr Thomas Lamplugh. They knew each other well, because Lamplugh had previously been Archdeacon of London and the Vicar of St-Martin-in-the-Fields, a church I knew from my previous visit to London, though I had not met him. This, Dr Compton assured me, was not surprising, since Dr Lamplugh was also Dean of Rochester at that time; indeed, he still was, since he had not surrendered the position when he assumed the office of Bishop of Exeter.

I had noted that this must involve him in much travelling, for Exeter and Rochester are separated by at least two hundred miles, but Dr Compton said that Lamplugh did not trouble himself too often with visiting either, preferring to maintain a house in London from which he could go to whichever place needed him if absolutely necessary. Compton asserted that Lamplugh did not choose to have this widely known, and preferred that people in Exeter should suppose that he was in Rochester, and those in Rochester that he was in Exeter. However, Compton knew that Lamplugh was in Exeter at that moment because it was a season of the year very dear to his heart, namely, the time that rents were due to him.

I had much to be grateful to Dr Compton for, and one great service that he had performed for me was to give an unvarnished — some might say, prejudicial — view of Dr Lamplugh's character. In the years that have passed since the events of which I write, I have come to the view that Compton was, if anything, excessively Christian when it came to Dr Lamplugh, but I hope that the reader will not think it amiss if I briefly explain here what happened after this time.

Lamplugh was a Jacobite; that is, he supported King James II, and since Compton did not one must allow for some bias. When the Archbishop of York died in 1686, the year after my tale, the King did not fill the vacancy for two years, but finally gave it to Lamplugh as a reward for his support and, it was said, his sympathy for the Roman Catholic faith. Unfortunately, Lamplugh had only just been confirmed when James fled and he was faced with a new, and very Protestant, monarch. Lamplugh therefore changed his opinions once more and was successful enough to die while still Archbishop.

Anyway, at the time of my story it was Compton's firm belief that Lamplugh was a staunch supporter of the King and could be relied upon to oppose any plan by the Duke of Monmouth to land in the West Country. For my purposes, this was ideal. If I could lose the letter in Exeter and it came into Lamplugh's hands, he would be certain to forward it to King James; and, coming from the hand of a loyal bishop, it would carry more credence than if I had handed it in at Whitehall myself.

My task was simply stated. I must meet the bishop, somehow convince him that the Duke of Monmouth had plans to land somewhere nearby, lose the letter that 'proved' the fact, and then go home as fast as the *Nieuwpoort* could take me. Simple, I thought.

I thought wrong.

The cart came to a halt at the City Quay. I had intended to stay aloft but my curiosity was piqued to see whether the water was deep enough to allow the *Nieuwpoort* to berth there. I had been alarmed by the suggestion that the channel might be barely half a fathom deep, so I climbed down to see for myself. Unfortunately, it was not easy to see, and so I asked an official-looking man how deep the water was there. To my delight, I could understand the answer. At the moment, he thought that it would be about seven feet deep, but nearer to thirty feet at high tide.

'Excellent!' I said. 'Then my ship will be able to dock here as planned.'

The man looked at me oddly as if to say that a traveller arriving by cart need not concern himself with the depth of a tidal river, and hurried away before I could explain, so I resumed my seat on the cart and we began to climb the gentle hill towards the cathedral which I could see not far distant. It seemed that the bishop's palace was hard by the cathedral rather than in the country as some bishops prefer.

I am bound to say that the cathedral and its environs are very comely indeed. A handsome close bounds it to one side where the dignitaries of the church live, and there is a fine area in front allowing an uncrowded view of the west end of the cathedral.

The carter drew up outside the palace door and waited until I had ascertained that the bishop was, indeed, at home. I was relying upon him for lodging for at least one night, otherwise I should have to return to the ship and bed down there. If the truth be told (as it should and must be) I was looking forward to a night in an immobile bed, ideally wider than an infant's arm-span across.

While I waited for someone to answer my knock I had time to observe that the palace had seen better days. The building itself was fine, but some of the windows were patched where glass had been broken and at least one window frame was not original, but had been replaced with an ill-matched alternative out of keeping with the age of the main fabric.

A servant appeared and raised an eyebrow. This, it seemed, substituted for any interrogative speech.

'My name is Master Mercurius of the University of Leiden in the United Provinces,' I said. 'I have a letter of introduction to the Bishop from the Bishop of London.'

The fellow accepted it between his thumb and forefinger as if I had given him a baby's soiled loincloth, and mutely indicated a chair in which I might sit. He crossed the hall in a stately, not to say ponderous, way and opened the door of a room that I took to be a study.

'Who? What?' said a voice petulantly.

'From the Bishop of London, Your Grace.'

'The Bishop of London? Why is he here?'

'A man sent by the Bishop, Your Grace. A German, I shouldn't wonder.'

I have been called many things in my time but I doubt that I have ever been so insulted.

'With a letter of introduction, Your Grace.'

'Well, give it here, man. Best offer him a glass of wine while I read it. But not the best stuff, d'you hear?'

The servant closed the door carefully and walked slowly across the hall once again. You might have thought he was officiating at a funeral to judge by his pace.

'His Grace is sorry to keep you waiting. Perhaps a glass of wine, sir?'

'Thank you, no,' I replied. If I was not to be offered the best stuff I preferred to have nothing at all.

'As you wish. If you will excuse me, then, I shall return to my duties.'

Whatever those duties were, I doubt they were attended to before bedtime, unless they were performed just around the corner.

In due course the door opened and a man of around seventy years appeared, well wrapped against the cold with a fur mantle over his shoulders.

'Forgive me, Master Mercurius,' he said. 'You have taken me unprepared, sir; but my brother bishop speaks very warmly of you, very warmly indeed, sir. I am sorry that this palace is not as comfortable as his but you are welcome anyway.'

'You are very kind, sir,' I replied. 'I am sorry to impose, and hope to conclude my business here very quickly.'

'You have business in Exeter?' the bishop asked, ushering me into his study.

I glanced about me. I have never been able to resist a library, though I could resist this one, since it seemed to be remarkably deficient in books. Lamplugh followed my gaze.

'The result of our civil war, Master. The palace was seized by the Parliamentarians after the late King Charles of blessed memory was martyred, and used for various profane purposes until his son restored it to us. But I am afraid that much was destroyed while it was out of our hands, and it will take many years to return the library to its former state.'

'I sympathise,' I said. And I did. It would break my heart to see a library that I frequented stripped of its books. Looking about me, I think my own poor shelves in Leiden might have been better stocked.

'Of course, as books of ours come to light I am not slow to reclaim them. But the thieves who have them do not advertise the fact; and I fear that many were destroyed.'

He offered me a chair, and I politely waited for him to sit first before following suit.

Lamplugh had a sad countenance, with a white moustache and a small chin beard. His eyes were dark and melancholy, and his cheeks reposed in such a way that his mouth turned down a little when at rest.

The room was chilly. A small fire burned in a grate, but the bishop rubbed his hands together to keep them warm and occasionally shrugged the fur higher on his shoulders. A draught whistled at a window behind him. I dreaded to think what the palace must be like in winter.

'I understand, sir, that you met the Bishop of London on a previous visit.'

'Yes, Your Grace. I was part of the Dutch delegation negotiating the marriage of William of Orange to Princess Mary some years ago.'

Lamplugh nodded slowly. 'It is, of course, not my place to criticise a member of the Royal Family...' he began, a sure sign that he was about to do just that, 'but it must be a great trial to

His Majesty to have a daughter who has shown herself so undutiful as to give comfort to His Majesty's enemies.'

I presumed that this was a reference to the presence of the Duke of Monmouth in our country, if indeed he was there, but it seemed to me to be manifestly unfair to Princess Mary. 'Surely, Your Grace, a woman's duty is to her husband, by whom she must be guided?'

'What? Oh, yes, it goes without saying. A wife cannot contend with her master.'

For some reason an image of my grandmother of blessed memory entered my head. I could not imagine her acknowledging my grandfather as her master. As she would tell me, the rider may hold the reins but a mare can still bolt.

'I am pleased to say,' I added, 'that Her Royal Highness is extremely popular in my homeland and is widely credited with being responsible for the state of amity now existing between us.'

'I am delighted to hear it, sir,' replied the bishop in a tone that clearly indicated that he did not believe it for one moment.

I had passed many hours rehearsing what I should say at this juncture. I need not say, I hope, that I had no intention of lying, which would be unbecoming in a clergyman, but perhaps I could express myself in such a way that I left open all manner of possibilities while saying something and nothing.

'Your Grace, knowing that true religion is the underpinning and source of security of any realm, my master the Stadhouder has sent me to discuss how our national churches might co-operate to their mutual benefit. The Bishop of London would welcome this, but, knowing that you and he were not always of one mind, suggested that I should seek an audience with you to receive the benefit of your opinion.'

Well, there were no actual lies in what I had said, but I do not know that I have ever crammed so many half-truths into a speech.

'Brother London is very kind,' Lamplugh remarked, preening himself that his opinions were given any weight by others. 'It is true that we do not always see things in the same light; and I remark, without wishing to labour the point, that during the lamentable time of the Commonwealth, when a reasonable man might have expected more friendship between the Reformed Church in the Low Countries and the Presbyterian Church exhibited here, relations sank further than ever.'

He had a point. Oliver Cromwell took exception to the fact that some of Charles I's family took refuge in our country. In our defence, since the current Stadhouder's father was married to Charles' sister, it was not surprising that the exiles sought shelter in our lands, but there was no doubt that it rankled with the English. It would have upset the Dutch even more had they known then, as they later discovered, that our rulers then had agreed with Cromwell to keep William forever from the Stadhoudership, a pledge that they had been obliged to abandon when he became an adult.

'Your Grace has a long memory,' I replied.

Lamplugh's lips twitched. I think it may have been a smile, or as close to one as he was capable of producing. 'A long memory is a great assistance in life, I find.'

I had the feeling that he was trying to convey some covert message in telling me that, as if he knew some dark secret that was not to my advantage, though, unless he had discovered the regrettable episode when I mouthed the answers to an examination to another boy at my Latin school, I could not imagine what it might be. [Van der Meer is shocked at this revelation, but no harm was done by it, since Brokamp, the boy concerned, was such a dunce that even when given the answers he wrote them next to the wrong questions. However, his father was very wealthy and the last I heard Brokamp was the mayor of some small town where, I imagine, he manages perfectly well without Latin — or, indeed, grammatical Dutch.]

Lamplugh rose from his chair, so I followed suit.

'If you'll excuse me, I will give orders to prepare a room and lay an extra place for supper, when we can continue our conversation. In the meantime, I must attend Evensong. No doubt you will wish to praise God too?'

'Of course,' I replied. When you're a minister of religion it doesn't do to say that you'd rather not bother to go to church; in fact, the service was delightful, with some excellent music provided by the choristers. The Dean gave the sermon, taking as his text Deuteronomy, chapter 22, verse 8: *When thou buildest a new house, then thou shalt make a battlement for thy roof, that thou bring not blood upon thine house, if any man fall from thence.* I had never preached on that passage before, and after hearing what the Dean made of it, I never will.

As we walked back to the Palace the bishop questioned me closely on my view of the sermon, and I gave as good an answer as I could given that English is not my best language. At first I could not understand his interest in my opinion, until I realised that he must have fallen asleep during those fifty minutes and did not wish to advertise the fact if anyone should ask him for a comment on it.

The table was set and we went in to supper, which consisted of a thick broth of some kind, a hash of hare and some white bread with excellent cheese. The bishop slurped his soup noisily, this being the fashion amongst the English, and plied me with a rough red wine, of which he had three goblets.

'Well, sir,' he said good-naturedly, 'now that you have experienced the English church at its finest, are you still minded to come closer to us?'

Several questions were wrapped up in this, but I judged the only proper answer was to declare my enthusiasm for closer union. 'However, there will remain some matters for further discussion,' I said, hoping that he would not ask me what they were. I just had a nasty feeling at the back of my neck about the fact that an understanding between the churches was the cover story for my visit, and I doubted very much that the Stadhouder had given any thought whatsoever to the reaction at home if I inadvertently achieved it. I was fairly sure that I would be burned in effigy in sundry places, not least of them being Leiden, a Reformed town if ever there was one. If I had admitted to listening to choral music in church at least one member of my own faculty would never speak to me again and would probably be the first to bring faggots to pile about my feet at the stake.

Fortunately the bishop took my note of caution for second thoughts and smiled that ghastly smile of his once more. 'Indeed, Master, indeed. Make haste slowly, eh?' He poured me another cup of wine to show his approbation of my comment. 'There remain,' he said in the manner of a schoolmaster, 'a number of theological and doctrinal issues that would require some elucidation. But the chief obstacle, I fear, is that His Majesty is strongly opposed to some Reformed novelties. He is a Catholic, you know.'

This last sentence was uttered *sotto voce* as if a great secret were being shared.

At this point I was compelled to stifle a yawn.

'My dear sir, I forget that you have travelled far and are doubtless weary. Perhaps you wish to retire?'

'I am feeling rather fatigued,' I admitted.

'Of course. Slow will show you to your chamber. Good night!'

The servant opened the door for me, and as I bade the bishop a good night in return he spoiled my night's sleep with just a few words.

'I'll see you at Mattins.'

CHAPTER SIXTEEN

I have known places where Mattins or morning prayer was said at dawn. I am pleased to say that Exeter was not one of them, so I was able to sleep in until seven o'clock. I could have slept much longer, given that my bed stayed still and it was sufficiently large to have accommodated a friend if I had brought one with me. After trying to sleep in what passed for a bed on board ship, it was luxurious. Needless to say, the room was freezing, partly because my arrival had been unexpected and it had obviously not occurred to Slow to set a fire while we were at Evensong. Instead, he started it as we were having supper, thus ensuring that when I retired for the night the chamber was still chilly but nevertheless smelt strongly of smoke. In the interests of domestic economy, there was only sufficient wood to keep it alight until I went to sleep; by the time I woke in the morning a snowman could have made himself very comfortable in the fireside chair.

I washed and dressed hurriedly and was just combing my hair when Slow arrived with the water for my shave, so I stripped back to my shirt to complete that task. If ever a man was well-named, it was Slow. By the time I had shaved, dressed again and gone downstairs Slow was still ambling towards the kitchen bearing what looked like the remains of breakfast.

'His Grace is gone before, sir,' Slow informed me.

'Am I very late, Slow?'

'Very late, sir? No, not *very* late. His Grace has just left. If you hurry you may overtake him.'

I grabbed a piece of bread and thanked him before chasing after the bishop who, to my great relief, was stopping every few steps to converse with various people. I caught up with him and we walked in together. The Dean greeted us and my heart initially sank at the prospect of another of his sermons, but it transpired that he was not preaching that morning.

The Dean was introduced to me as Mr Annesley, but I discovered that he was actually The Honourable Richard Annesley, being the son of an Earl. Although he had the appearance of middle age, he was in fact barely thirty years old. As the bishop left us to take his seat in a large, ornate chair, the Dean and I continued to talk. I explained my mission, and to my surprise the Dean was markedly enthusiastic.

'I fear, sir, that His Majesty's present course, if continued, will lead to further strife amongst us,' he explained.

'Perhaps His Majesty is being poorly advised,' I suggested.

'It wouldn't matter who advised him,' said the Dean, 'for he never listens to them.'

I was surprised that a senior clergyman would be so free with his comments about the Supreme Head of the established church.

'His Majesty is a brave man,' the Dean continued. 'I do not impugn his courage. But he is not favoured with extensive intelligence. He demonstrates his willingness never to shirk a battle by generating more of them.'

'His Grace the Bishop seems to think well of him,' I mused.

'Yes,' agreed the Dean. 'That speaks volumes.'

Not to me, it didn't. I had no idea what he meant.

When the service was over I walked back with the bishop to collect my things before taking my leave. 'May I say to my Master that you are not averse to greater links with our church, Your Grace?' I asked him.

Lamplugh paused to consider the matter before replying guardedly. 'Say rather that I am keen to live in peace and friendship with all so far as my vow to my Sovereign permits.'

In England those who are ordained priests must swear an oath of allegiance to the King, so it was understandable that Lamplugh could not be seen to be doing anything that was not in line with that vow, but it seemed a little mealy-mouthed to me, as if he wanted me to think that he supported the union of the churches whereas in fact he was only prepared to do so when there was no chance that it would happen; a little like William's support for Monmouth's invasion, come to think of it.

I thanked him for his hospitality and took my leave of him. Since Hendriks had said that the ship would be at the City Quay no later than lunchtime, I thought I would see something of the city, lose that confounded letter somewhere, and board the *Nieuwpoort* in the early afternoon for the return journey.

It was then that I had a stroke of luck. Walking away from the cathedral, I saw a low alley leading to the centre of the city, and on one side was a tavern which proudly declared itself to be a favourite drinking haunt of Sir Francis Drake. This man Drake was a famous English sailor, though some kind of licensed pirate; but the English are very proud of his exploits, so I thought that it was the sort of tavern that would attract English naval officers. If I were to lose the letter there, it would be discovered after I was gone and the naval officers would vouch for its authenticity and ensure that it was taken to the right people to set William's plan in motion. Accordingly, I pushed open the door and stepped inside.

Everyone turned to look at me, so I touched my hat and bade them a good day. The innkeeper poured me a beaker of ale and helped me to understand the little English money I had so that I could pay for it, and I am pleased to say that such was his honesty that I was only overcharged by around half of what I was overcharged in London.

I judged it best to sit in some dark corner where I was not easily observed in case some meddling fool spotted me leaving the letter and insisted on returning it to me, so I found a high-sided chair and discreetly fumbled inside my shirt for the letter. Checking that I was not being observed I slipped it against the wood to one side and trapped it there with my hip. The temptation to leave at once was very powerful, but instead I drank my beer at an unhurried pace.

A potboy appeared as I set my beaker down and asked if I wanted more.

'Thank you,' I said, 'but I have to go. I have a boat waiting for me.'

The boy, ten or twelve years old, listened intently to me. 'You'd be a foreign gentleman, I'd say.'

'I'm Dutch,' I replied.

'We don't get many Dutchies in here,' he said. 'And never vicars.'

'I'm a minister of the Dutch Reformed Church.' I thought it was best to leave it at that.

'You're a long way from home, sir.'

'I'm here on business on behalf of my master the Stadhouder.'

'The what?'

'The Stadhouder. He's rather like our King.'

William was not actually a King, but nobody had plucked up the courage to tell him that yet.

'Jack!' bellowed the innkeeper, and the boy rushed to attend upon him, which gave me the opportunity to check that the letter was still jammed in the side of the chair, gather my hat and leave.

The urge to go sightseeing had quitted me, because if there was any chance that Hendriks had arrived early there was a possibility that we might leave early too. I did not want to miss a favourable tide, so I set out to walk to the City Quay. Desiring to take the shortest route, I stopped a well-dressed man beside the cathedral and asked directions to the quay, which he gave me, and, following his arm movements (because his speech was near to incomprehensible) I passed through an arch and into a broad lane, turning right towards the river.

It was a pleasant enough day, if a little colder than I had expected, and I was struck by the friendliness of the local women, several of whom spoke to me. They seemed to want to know if I had the time, which I did not, since I do not carry a watch, and a couple offered to walk with me, but I had to decline their kind offer for fear that they would slow me down.

I arrived at the quay and looked about for any sign of the *Nieuwpoort* but could see none. I scrutinised each of the ships there to see if any were Dutch but to no avail, and then I saw a small hut with a sign declaring it to be the pilot's office. The pilot would know how things stood, I thought, because one would be needed to bring the ship upriver to the quay so someone there would be able to tell me when the *Nieuwpoort* was expected.

I pushed open the door to reveal two men smoking their pipes. One was writing in a large book while the other appeared to have no useful employment.

'I wonder if you can help me,' I said. 'I came to Topsham yesterday and my ship was expected to come upriver on the next tide to collect me at the quay.'

The man who was writing turned to look at me. 'Ah! You'd be the Dutch gent as took the cart into town.'

'That's right,' I agreed. 'And you must have been the pilot who greeted us.'

'The very same, sir.'

'So when is the *Nieuwpoort* expected?'

'It isn't.'

'It isn't? But I don't understand. They were supposed to come for me here.'

The man stabbed the air with the stem of his pipe. 'I thought the very same, sir. Didn't I say, Jem, as I thought it was odd?'

'You did, Obadiah, you did,' agreed his companion.

'What was odd?' I asked.

'Why, that having had their orders from you, they should put me back in the row-boat and head out to sea without delay. Mind, they paid me my fee, so I've no complaint, but I thought to myself "Obadiah," I thought, "that clergyman is going to be spitting mad when he finds they've gone without him, and him not knowing a soul in Exeter." And it seems I was right to think so.'

'So you were,' agreed Jem. "Tain't right to cast a man ashore so to fend for himself.'

'Let me get this right,' I pleaded. 'You say the *Nieuwpoort* sailed without me.'

'That's the long and the short of it.'

'She couldn't be berthed again at Topsham?'

'Not without I was called again to her, sir. But don't take my word for it. I must stay at my post, but Jem here would gladly row you downriver to see for yourself. At a price.'

Jem indicated his willingness to do as offered.

'It seems I have no choice,' I answered. At least I might find out what Hendriks' plans were. Had he been unable to secure a berth? Perhaps he had seen something he needed to investigate, or an English ship had threatened the *Nieuwpoort* or shown too much interest in it.

Jem held out his hand and I placed a coin in it, at which he seemed highly satisfied, and led the way to a small boat. I am not a mariner, as the alert reader will have deduced, but as I climbed into the boat it seemed to me that there was a lot of water about our feet.

'Hitch up your gown, sir, and I'll deal with that,' said Jem, and used a wooden bowl to scoop water over the side before handing it to me. 'If it troubles us again, sir, perhaps you'd be so kind…'

He was a practised rower and soon we were gliding along in response to his long pulls at the oars. It would have been quite a pleasant excursion down the river if it were not cold, I had not had the prospect of desertion on my mind and the river had stayed outside the boat rather than creeping in through gaps in the boards. I was so busy baling that I did not at first realise that we had arrived at Topsham.

'Will you come with me, Jem?' I asked, knowing that I had difficulty comprehending the local speech.

Jem dragged the boat clear of the water and tied it up, taking an age over the whole exercise, but at length we entered the inn and I was able to ask the innkeeper if he knew what had become of the *Nieuwpoort*.

'They've gone to Exeter to collect you,' he replied.

'That they haven't,' Jem protested, 'for we would know and we've just come from there.'

'Well, they said as they was…'

'They may have said, but they didn't,' Jem argued.

The innkeeper rubbed his chin. 'I suppose that explains why they went that-a-way first.' He pointed out to sea.

'They left me?' I stammered.

'So it seems,' agreed the innkeeper.

I will not deny that a number of thoughts crowded my brain at this point, not all of them charitable or Christian. I was determined that William should hear of this dereliction of duty, but first I had to get back to The Hague to tell him of it.

'Do Dutch ships come here often?' I asked.

'Oh, yes!' cried the innkeeper. 'One came only a year or two back.'

If I was going to return to my homeland I needed to return to London. I had some money, so perhaps I could take a stagecoach from Exeter. The bishop was a regular visitor to London; he would know what my options were.

'Jem,' I said reluctantly, 'I must return to Exeter. Will you row me?'

He touched his cap with his finger in agreement and held out his hand for the fare.

When I was a young man I found ideas easy to come by. I would sit in the library reading a book, and as I was still reading a multiplicity of notions would leap into my head; and within a few moments objections to some of them would come forth, and I would find those that were most likely to bear fruit pushing to the front. As I have matured, my thoughts have become more prudent and cautious, and I try to have one at a time and deal with it fully before allowing a second to appear. As a result I had come upon my middle years uncertain as to whether my brain would ever again function at the lightning speed of my youth.

As I sat in Jem's boat I had my answer. Ideas and plans blazed in and out of sight but always with the problem that there was one unknowable quantity that remained unknowable.

If I considered what Hendriks was up to, I could not know what had caused him to move and thus vary our original agreement. If I turned my mind to what had happened to Velders, I could not think why he should betray his trust, except that the love of money is at the root of all evil, but then I had to think how unlikely it was that someone would attack Velders just after he had taken possession of my letter, unless, of course, we were being watched, in which event it must be someone on the ship, but then why not assault Velders on board? Why wait until we berthed? The only answer I could think of was that there was no possibility of escape from a ship at sea, but if it was one of the sailors then why had they all stayed on the ship, for none had deserted? And, from all I understood, none of them could leave the ship without leave of the captain, and none had been given that at the relevant time.

For no sensible reason, I kept looking about me as if there was the remotest chance that the *Nieuwpoort* would come into view, having been hiding behind a tree or concealed behind some smaller boat, though I knew that to be impossible. How was I going to explain to William that I had lost his favourite ship? Or, more likely, what story would the sailors spin to explain why they had returned without me? Of course, I would return to my homeland eventually. If I could get to London, which was probably around a fortnight's walk, I was sure to find a ship to the United Provinces sooner or later.

I closed my eyes and pictured the scene as I arrived at the Binnenhof, demanded entry and dramatically marched into the great hall. All the heads would turn, betraying their astonishment that I was still alive. William would step forward to embrace me like the father kissing the Prodigal Son in the gospel parable, before slapping me on both cheeks and demanding "Where is my ship?"

My head jolted.

'Forgive me, Master,' said Jem, 'but you was a-sleeping and we need you to keep baling the water out.'

I set to with the bowl and around half an hour later we approached the quay, where I could see signs of consternation. Obadiah could be seen summoning a boy and sending him on an errand, no doubt to tell the bishop that I was returned and would need lodging.

We moored at the end of a small jetty and I clambered up to the quay, accepting the hand of a man who helped me up. To my surprise, he did not let me go when once I was set on dry land, but held me by the elbow. The crowd parted and I found myself looking at four large men with heavy staffs, and, in front of them, the potboy from the inn I had visited earlier.

'That's him,' said the lad. 'That's the Dutchie spy.'

CHAPTER SEVENTEEN

To say that I was nonplussed by this turn of events would be something of an understatement. Viewing my actions as dispassionately as I could, I might concede that one or two aspects of my behaviour might have aroused some suspicion amongst ignorant observers but, as my readers will know, there were perfectly good explanations for all of them. Well, almost all of them.

I tried to persuade the constables, for that is what those four large men were, that if they would only allow me to speak to the bishop all would be set aright, but they told me that he did not wish to see me, besides which, he was the person who had set them on me.

I do not have great experience of the English legal system, nor of our own, for that matter, but I soon realised that it has a great defect insofar as the accused has trouble getting a fair hearing. I could not persuade anyone to tell me exactly what accusation was being levelled against me, nor the evidence on which it was based; and to my protestations of innocence they simply replied "Well, you would say that, wouldn't you?"

I offered no physical resistance to being led away to see the magistrate, though I objected mightily to being abused and pelted with rotten vegetables by passers-by. I ask you, what kind of person goes around with rotten fruit about their person just in case they come across someone who needs pelting? Admittedly in England there always seems to be someone in the stocks or pillory, but if he is a notorious evil-liver they may throw rocks and if he is a much-loved local character the missiles are more likely to be small loaves in case he has not had breakfast. Since the locals can have had no more idea of the charges against me than I had myself I can only assume that they chuck things at anyone in the constables' keeping on the assumption that they must have done something reprehensible to deserve arrest.

We arrived at the Guildhall. It is an imposing building, said to be above three hundred years old, with an impressive frontage supported on pillars. The large chamber juts into the street and there are stocks directly under it, which has the merit of convenience for the malefactor, who is spared a long walk. I was led inside and pushed up the stairs to the large chamber where a man was dictating letters to a clerk.

The man briefly looked up and then looked again more closely.

'Upon my word, a parson! What cause brings him here, Serjeant?'

'Plotting against the King's Peace, Mayor.'

'Treason!'

'Not treason, sir, for he is a Dutchie.'

'Spying then. Well, bring him here, and let us consider the evidence. Foreigner or no, he must have a fair trial before he is hanged.'

The Mayor, Robert Dabynott, waved the clerk away. 'Letters later. Peace of the realm first.' He pointed to a chair. 'In deference to his cloth, I'll interview him seated.'

That was obviously the only deference I could expect, because the villains roughly pushed me down on the chair. I carefully arranged my robe which had become disordered.

'Do you speak English?' Dabynott yelled slowly.

I resisted the temptation to point out the illogicality of expecting an answer from anyone who did not; it seemed neither the time nor the place and might only serve to annoy him. 'A little, sir,' I replied. Calling people sir is never a bad move when they have the upper hand over you.

'Your name?'

'I am Master Mercurius of the University of Leiden.'

'Write that down,' Dabynott instructed his clerk. 'No, man, on a fresh sheet of paper!' He eyed me carefully. 'A parson of some kind.'

'A minister of God, yes.' Let us not go into exactly what kind of minister, I thought. That tends to get complicated.

'Your business here?'

'I was sent by the Prince of Orange to discuss church affairs with the Bishop of London, who in turn sent me to the Bishop of Exeter.'

Dabynott seemed to view this as entirely understandable, as if no serious matters in the land could be undertaken without consulting the Bishop of Exeter. 'Have you spoken to His Grace?'

'Yes! I only left his company this morning. He can vouch for me.'

If only that inept wretch Velders had not mistakenly stolen my letter of accreditation I could have produced it now and saved myself a great deal of trouble. If I found myself in London again I had a good mind to speak severely to him, whether he could hear me or no.

'I doubt the Bishop would speak for him, Mayor,' the Serjeant chipped in, 'since it was him that told us to arrest the foreign gent, only he had attempted to flee the country.'

'I didn't flee,' I protested. 'I took a boat in search of my ship.'

'Which ship would that be?' Dabynott asked.

'The *Nieuwpoort*,' I answered. 'It brought me here.'

'No such ship docked here, Mayor,' said the Serjeant, at which one of the constables mumbled words of agreement. 'Matthew here works at the Quay and knows all the comings and goings.'

'It left me at Topsham,' I explained.

'Why at Topsham, since your business was in Exeter?' Dabynott enquired, squinting slightly to look more incisive in his questioning.

'I don't know. Something to do with the tides.'

'They'm the same tides here as at Topsham,' the man Matthew volunteered. ''Tis the same water. If the tide's out at Exeter it's out at Topsham too.'

'Aha!' Dabynott thundered. 'Got you there, Dutchie!'

'I am not a sailor,' I explained patiently. 'I do not know the reason. I only know that the captain took us to Topsham, where the ship would have to wait for the next tide. I was in haste, so I was brought to Exeter by cart.'

'And you presented yourself at the Bishop's Palace?'

'Yes.'

'No, begging your pardon, Mayor, but first he went about the Quay asking questions about ships and the depth of water there,' the Serjeant interjected.

'That's suspicious,' Dabynott said. 'Checking our defences, I shouldn't wonder.'

'I was only trying to see if the *Nieuwpoort* would be able to dock there to collect me. I didn't ask questions about ships.'

'We have witnesses,' said the Serjeant.

I replayed as much of the conversation to myself as I could. What could I possibly have said? 'If I mentioned ships, it would only have been small talk,' I expostulated. 'What else is there to talk about at a dock?'

'Aha! So first you deny that you spoke of ships, then you allow that you might have done. See, sir, how your story falls apart!'

I have never been a mayor, nor wanted to be. They seem to me to be middle-aged, self-satisfied men, who have made sufficient money to be able to devote some time to doing whatever it is that mayoring involves. I sometimes want to explain to my fellow citizens that having a lot of money does not guarantee intelligence, not even when they made that money themselves.

'Bring that potboy forward,' ordered Dabynott.

The boy, being brought, swiftly removed his cap and clutched it in front of his heart as if in awe of this portly merchant.

'Tell the Mayor what you told me,' urged the Serjeant.

'Well, sir, this gentleman came in to the inn where I work, The Ship, bold as brass and takes a seat. Then he drinks a pot of ale. Then he goes.'

That seemed to me to be a pretty fair summary of things, but the interfering Serjeant wanted more.

'Tell the Mayor about the letter.'

'Oh, yes, sir. When he'd gone I found a letter jammed down the side of the chair where he'd been sitting. I chased after him to return it, but I couldn't see him.'

'So what did you do?' asked the Mayor in that tone of voice that adults use to children when they want to pretend that they are taking them seriously.

'I gave the letter to my master the innkeeper, because I don't have the reading, so that we might discover where to return it.'

'And what did the innkeeper do?'

'Why, he opened it, sir, saying there was no other way to know where to deliver it.'

'He opened my letter?' I gasped. My astonishment was purely that a man would open another man's letter, you understand, but it was rapidly misconstrued.

'Aha! See, you are undone! It is as well this true Englishman opened it so your devilry was laid bare,' the Mayor announced, to a general nodding of heads. 'Perhaps now, Master Mercurius — if indeed you are Master Mercurius — you will reveal the contents of the letter and throw yourself on our mercy.'

'It was a sealed letter,' I pointed out. 'How should I know the contents of it?'

The Serjeant stepped forward and produced my letter. 'See, the seal has been smudged over to conceal the sender. And the letter within is damning.'

The Mayor opened the letter and read it carefully. I could see that this was not going well for me because his cheeks moved from red to purple. The best I could hope for was that he would die of an apoplexy before uttering a word of condemnation. 'These are plans for an invasion of England by the treacherous Duke of Monmouth!' exclaimed Dabynott. 'The Lord be praised that they have fallen into our hands.'

'Now that we have cleared that up, may I go?' I asked.

'Go, sir? No, sir, you will not leave and tell the Duke that his plans are discovered. We will send these to the King and no doubt a trap will be laid for your master the Duke, who will rue the day he took up arms against the rightful King of England, as will you.'

Anyone who has seen me attempt to pick up a sword will know that nobody has need to fear me if I take up arms against them. Swords are remarkably heavy and some are extremely sharp. A man could hurt himself with the edge of one.

'No, sir, you are bound for the dungeons, there to await His Majesty's pleasure. I expect you'll be there until the next

Assizes, when Judge Jeffreys will send you a good deliverance from jail at the end of a rope.'

This was an unwelcome outcome and I will not deny that I was mightily vexed at my situation. I rapidly tried to think of anyone who might be able to offer me some relief. 'If I might write to the Bishop of London, he will vouch for me,' I said.

'No doubt he would, for he is no friend of His Majesty the King,' Dabynott answered. 'We should be grateful that Exeter at least has a bishop of undoubted loyalty to His Majesty.'

I was yanked out of the chair and pushed towards the door. Rough arms grabbed me and dragged me to a small flight of stairs which led to an underground chamber. A key was produced, the door thrown open, and I was flung inside. I had just managed to right myself when the room was pitched into near darkness as the heavy oak door was closed and I heard the key turned in the lock.

Well, I thought, *this isn't going quite to plan.*

If the victuals at the Bishop's Palace were rather rustic, those in the dungeon were positively vile. By the time two meals had passed I was pining for Albrecht's cooking, which just shows how the balance of my mind was disturbed by my captivity. I did not eat much of the first, though I might have returned to it after an hour or so if I had not seen a rat making off with some of it. There were several such creatures in the dungeon, and one of them appeared to be showing a profound and unwelcome interest in my toes, so I hurried to ensure that my shoes were on my feet at all times.

The Serjeant was also my jailer, and was attentive enough to pass by my door every hour or so to abuse me as the foulest villain Exeter had ever known. He also kept up a running commentary on my situation, which is how I know some of what follows.

My letter had, it seemed, been enclosed in one from the Mayor in which he claimed the credit for uncovering a fiendish plot against the King, and sent to London by the afternoon mail-coach. By the Serjeant's reckoning the coach would be in London by the following afternoon, since it continued on its way by night, so we might expect orders for my trial and inevitable execution within three or four days.

My spirits were low. I sank to my knees and prayed as fervently as ever I did, but no answer came, and it began to weigh upon me that St Paul died in prison, and that Saints Peter and Andrew were both executed, and all these were holier men than me. If God had not relieved them of their suffering, why should he do so for me?

There was a small window bearing an iron grille high in the wall opposite the door, far too elevated for me to see out but ideally placed for rain and wind to come in. I also discovered that the young bucks of the town were in the habit of relieving themselves there when they knew a prisoner might be seated below it. Fortunately, as a clergyman I had not been shackled to the wall, so I was able to shuffle around a bit. What little light entered there was insufficient to tell me what time of day it was, except that for an hour or so each day there was more light than at other times. I did not have my travelling bag and therefore was deprived of my books also, whereupon I discovered that despite saying the offices of the day diligently every day for many years I could not remember them precisely by heart; and if I prayed incorrectly I beg God's pardon. He will understand that I was under some strain. After all, I had never been hanged before, but I was fairly sure that it would not be a pleasurable experience. I had not watched an execution — if required to be there I always close my eyes at key moments — but witnesses were unanimous that the criminal always struggled mightily and that his gasps as he attempted to breathe were always terrible to hear.

By the end of the second day my spirits had declined so far that I found myself weeping in the most unmanly fashion, so that the Serjeant had compassion on me, and offered to pray a while with me; upon my consenting thereto, he produced a Prayer Book and began to read certain verses of Psalm Thirty-nine: "Lord, let me know mine end, and the number of my days: that I may be certified how long I have to live. Behold, thou hast made my days as it were a span long: and mine age is even as nothing in respect of thee; and verily every man living is altogether vanity."

That evening the Serjeant brought my meal himself. It consisted of a lump of coarse bread and some scraps of pork fat which he seemed to esteem a great delicacy, smacking his lips as he drew attention to them. He also produced a large flask of wine.

'If you've got any money I can get some you luxuries to make your stay here more enjoyable,' he announced breezily.

'Luxuries? You mean things like soap and edible food?'

'Compared with what my other prisoners get you're doing very well,' he replied in a hurt tone. 'I could take away your privileges and see if you notice if you like.'

'I'm sorry,' I answered. 'I'm rather tense. It's making me ungrateful.'

'Of course,' the Serjeant said sympathetically. 'It can't be easy to contemplate your untimely end dangling from a rope far from home. It would depress any man's spirits.' He poured me a cup of wine. 'If I were you I'd spend as much of the time drunk as you can,' he said. 'It'll make the time pass quicker, and if the order for your hanging comes while you're in your cups it'll be more pleasant for you anyway. With any luck you won't know what's happening as we fix the noose about you.'

I am not a violent man, but I hefted the flask in my hand to test what damage it might do to a man's skull before realising that such an action would assuredly damn me for all time, whereas unearned suffering is redemptive and being hanged in this world for something that I had not done might be to my advantage in the next. At least, I hoped it might be.

Whatever solace there might have been in the wine was being diminished by the Serjeant, who was liberally helping himself. I thought to encourage this in the hope that he would fall asleep and I might then abstract the key and let myself out. I had no idea where I would go, what I would do, or how I would get back to Leiden, but I could cross those bridges when I came to them.

While I was tossing this over in my mind the Serjeant suddenly lunged forward with his dagger. I thought my end was come, but when he resumed his seat I could see that he had impaled one of the rats.

'Nasty little buggers,' he said. 'I can't abide rats.'

'Thank you,' I answered. 'There are several others if you'd like to serve them likewise.'

'They come inside when it's cold,' he mumbled.

'You mean it's actually colder out there than it is in here?'

'Oh, yes! Less wind here, you see. That wind fair cuts through a man.' He glanced up at the sky, a small portion of which could just be seen above the building opposite. 'We shall have snow, I shouldn't wonder. Late in the year, but the winters have been murderous cruel lately.'

I gathered my thoughts. Could I turn this conversation to my advantage somehow? 'Mr Serjeant,' I said, 'I know appearances are against me, but I am innocent. You know that the letter was sealed.'

'You mean to say that you had no knowledge of what was within?' he asked.

Now, my protestations of innocence clearly required me to say that I did not; but, as the alert reader (if any) will know, I did know the contents. Ever since I was a boy I have been unable to lie without immediately giving myself away. If I try my cheeks colour and I usually end up contradicting myself and admitting my untruthfulness. I had ensnared myself unless I could think quickly.

Fortunately, quick thinking is something I have been schooled in for many years, and I was able to come up with a form of words that, while truthful, may have been misleading. At least, I hoped it was. 'I give you my word that I had not seen the contents,' I said.

The Serjeant took another slug of wine. 'I believe you,' said he. Rising to his feet, he handed me the flask. 'When they hang you, it'll be monstrous unjust,' he announced, letting himself out and locking the door behind him.

CHAPTER EIGHTEEN

A day or two later my spirits were even lower. Word had come from the King that I was to be held until the next Assizes, when the Lord Chancellor himself would come to Exeter to deal with me. I was in no hurry to meet this man Jeffreys, but neither did I wish to remain incarcerated for any long time. However I looked at it, my condition was desperate.

I was sitting on the floor feeling sorry for myself when a strange hallucination came over me. I could have sworn I could hear someone whistling; and clearly my senses were leaving me, because I knew the tune.

I am no singer, but it relieved my spirits to hear so cheerful a refrain and I joined in, remembering the words as best I could. It was a song called "Wat zal men op den avondt doen" — what shall men do in the evening? — which I had heard many times. There were a number of tunes, but that I had guessed rightly was demonstrated when another voice joined me from above. Was this an angel singing with me?

And then it stopped, and all was melancholy silence.

I tried to pick up the tune again, but tears came, and it was impossible. What was I to do in the evening except sit in my cell night after night until I was launched into eternity? Thus ran my thoughts, and I was so deep in them that I did not at first hear the whisper from above.

'Mercurius! Master Mercurius! Is that you?'

'Yes!' I whispered, probably a little too loudly.

'Quieter, man! I want you to keep away from this wall. Can you do that?'

'I suppose so. But it's the only light part of my cell.'

'There'll be light enough soon,' the voice said, and then was gone.

I had a faint notion that the voice was somehow familiar, but I could not place it. It certainly was not the Stadhouder, who was incapable of whispering; nor was it the Ambassador, nor Hendriks. Yet whoever he was, he spoke to me in Dutch.

The evening meal was brought, and I had heard no more, and could only think that my fevered brain had imagined the whole thing, when I saw a metal hook come in at the window and rotate until it grabbed a bar. A second hook, very like the first, soon followed. I could hear the clop of hooves on the cobbles outside, but was unprepared for the noise of an animal in pain. Suddenly the hooks were pulled away from me and a chisel blasted into the stonework. A second bleat of pain followed and there was some more chiselling, then with a loud crack the stone split and two of the bars flew from their places, creating a small hole.

A rope was dropped through the hole and the voice spoke again. 'Grab it and climb up!'

'I can't,' I protested.

'If you don't the next rope you see will be round your neck.'

This incentive worked mightily on me, and I found that I could indeed climb the rope; and while I would have sworn that the hole was too small for me to get through, I soon wriggled one shoulder and my head, then the second shoulder, and then by degrees the rest of me through the gap. I do not remember the circumstances of my birth but I believe I now know what an infant feels like at that time.

I lay on the wet street, exhausted by my efforts, but was roughly pulled to my feet.

'You can rest later,' I was told.

I could not discern his features in the poor light, but in any event my attention was drawn to a bull and the largest carthorse I had ever seen. My rescuer cut the ropes tying them to the hooks and smacked each on the backside, causing them to run off through the town.

'That should create enough of a distraction for our purposes,' he announced.

'Where did you get them?' I enquired.

'The market. No doubt they will return to their owners. But come, there is no time to waste. Follow me!' Taking my hand he led me through an alley.

'Isn't the river the other way?' I asked.

'Yes, but that's where they'll expect you to head. We are bound in the opposite direction, out of town and towards the moors.'

I might have questioned the wisdom of this had I not been so grateful to be saved from the noose.

'It's a shame I couldn't get your bag,' my rescuer said. 'You stink. A blind mongrel could follow your scent.'

'I'm very sorry,' I remarked with some asperity. 'I'd have bathed if I'd known you were coming to rescue me. Thank you, by the way.'

'You're welcome. It's what I'm paid for.'

All I could see by the dim starlight was that my rescuer was the sailor with the beard who had pretended to be a barber-surgeon. How he came to be in Exeter was beyond me, but I was grateful for his presence, and since he seemed to know what he was doing, I was keen to follow his instructions to the minutest detail.

We came to the city gate. Now, the city wall of Exeter was not in a good state, and it soon became clear that we were not going to leave by the gate when there was an alternative. Just to the west of the gate a couple of small huts had been erected, and above one of them the top of the wall was crumbling. While doubtless effective from the outside, it was not too difficult to scale from the inside, even for a novice like me. My guide clambered onto the roof and held down his hand.

'Climb on the other one to spread our weight. Then, when I gain the top of the wall, hop over to this and follow me. It's quite a drop on the other side, so hang from the top by your hands to reduce your fall. And when you let go, push yourself outwards so you don't land in the stinking ditch.'

I did exactly as I was told, and he was right; it was quite a drop. I had my eyes closed as I pushed off the wall and thought for a moment that I was never going to land, but my feet hit the grass and I rolled backward before getting to my feet and heading for the nearest clump of trees with my rescuer.

We slumped in the bracken and I could happily have gone to sleep but my companion counselled against it.

'If they use dogs we may yet be found,' he explained. 'We need to get across a wide stream or river.' He scoured the sky for some particular star and, from this, determined that we needed to head in a certain direction.

'Where are we going?' I asked.

'Back to the *Nieuwpoort*.'

'You know where it is?'

'Yes. Or, more accurately, I know where Wilkens said he would take it.'

'Wilkens?'

'Yes.'

'Not Hendriks?'

There was a long silence before my rescuer spoke again. 'Mercurius, I know I'm a master of disguise but surely even you…'

A horrible thought came to me. 'You — you don't play the lute by any chance?'

He smiled, but said nothing.

'Beniamino? Is that you?'

I had hoped never to see this bragging fellow again. Of course, that was before I found myself in a dungeon waiting for a noose, after which I would have accepted help from the Devil himself.

'It is.'

'But…'

I could not think of the questions that I wanted him to answer. They were too many.

For those fortunate readers who have not encountered Beniamino before, allow me to explain that he was employed by the Stadhouder as a torture master and spy, and I was indebted to him already because he had saved my life when I was subjected to an attack with murderous intent in Utrecht in 1674. I had managed to avoid crossing his path for over ten years, and I can honestly say that during the whole of that time I did not miss him one little bit.

I will allow that to some extent his bold personality was an act, or part of his disguise. It was possible that he was not, in fact, as cavalier in his approach to the female sex as he presented; it may be that even when torturing people on the Stadhouder's behalf he did so reluctantly and only to the minimum necessary to discover the required information. It was also possible that he could play the lute tolerably well, despite appearances (though I very much doubted it) and that he may have known some songs which would not have caused the most hardened whore to blush. Beniamino liked to disguise himself as an itinerant lute-player, because musicians are anonymous and unnoticed; they can sit in a corner of the room strumming away while men talk treason, and since Beniamino claimed to be Italian and to have only a limited grasp of Dutch people spoke freely near him. Needless to say, he spoke Dutch as well as I did, and his name was not Beniamino, though he declined to provide any other.

'Better for us both if you don't know otherwise,' he would say, and for my part, if there was any physical peril attached to knowing his name I was very content to stick to Beniamino.

'So how do you come to be my guardian angel once again?' I enquired.

Beniamino ignored my question and stood up. 'Can you walk and talk at the same time?' he asked.

'Of course.'

'I forgot, you're a university man. They probably taught you to do that. Well, let's do so then. I'll feel happier when we break the scent trail.'

We trudged on in the dark, and after about half an hour we came across a broad stream. When I say "came across" I really mean "fell in", because I stepped in it and then slipped on wet stones.

Beniamino offered me his hand. 'Don't get out opposite where you fell in. We'll walk in the water a way to confuse any dogs. A couple of hundred paces should do the trick.'

'I'm soaking wet,' I protested.

'Then you can't get any wetter by staying in the water,' he replied. 'Whereas I was perfectly dry, but such is my love for you that I voluntarily got my boots wet. After all, I'm not the one they're chasing.'

I had to admit he had a point, but I had a better one. 'I expect the Stadhouder has given you the task of delivering me home safely, and would be displeased if you abandoned me.'

'I'm sure he would, but you know the Stadhouder. How long would he keep you in his thoughts once you were dead?'

That was a cruel remark, but sadly all too accurate. William, though estimable in many ways, tended to measure men's worth by their usefulness to him, and a dead man is not much help to a ruler.

I changed the subject. 'How far must we walk?'

'It's around thirty miles.'

'Thirty miles? I'm not sure I can manage that.'

'Think yourself lucky. I've already walked it in the opposite direction, though I ran some in the hope of arriving before you were hanged.'

'I'm grateful. But I meant that after a poor diet and a small cell I'm weaker than usual.'

Beniamino stopped. 'Are you hungry?' he asked.

'Very.'

He reached into a pouch on his belt and broke something in two, giving me one half. 'Ship's biscuit. For goodness' sake don't try to chew it until it's been softening in your mouth a few minutes.'

Biscuit is what sailors eat when they cannot have fresh bread, and having tasted it I now know why there are so many mutinies at sea. It sits in your mouth rather like a piece of roof tile, but if you worry away at it with your tongue and roll it around in your saliva eventually a little liquid will begin to soften the broken edge and, by degrees, it becomes more like a piece of poorly-tanned leather.

Beniamino indicated a point at which we might resort to the bank so I climbed out of the water and we plodded on.

'So you were on the *Nieuwpoort* all along?' I asked.

'I joined at the last moment. The usual barber-surgeon was persuaded that he didn't want to make the voyage.'

'Persuaded?'

'Relax. I didn't harm him. He was paid well to stay at home.'

'So did Velders know you were there to look after me?'

Beniamino winced. 'No. In retrospect, it would have been better if he had. He wouldn't have been hurt if he'd left it to me.'

I was puzzled, and fell to silence while I turned this over in my mind. Some time must have passed before enlightenment struck, because the first rays of dawn were visible ahead of us when I suddenly realised what a complete and utter dunce I had been. 'Velders didn't steal the letter from me!' I exclaimed.

'Have you only just worked that out?' retorted Beniamino.

'I was sure... I mean, he was the only person who knew about the letter I was carrying.'

'And how did he know?'

'The Stadhouder told him.'

'And how good is the Stadhouder at speaking in a low voice?'

'Someone overheard?'

'Yes, they did.'

I scratched my head in perplexity; possibly due to jail-fleas as well, but definitely in perplexity. 'Who?'

'Work it out,' Beniamino smiled. 'You're the famous investigator, not me.'

I thought feverishly. In the end my choice was ludicrously simple. 'It can't be Wilkens, because you've left him in charge of the ship, so it must be Hendriks.'

'Hurrah! At last!'

'But he searched so diligently for the letter when I lost it.'

'Of course he did. How could he not, without giving the game away?'

'But he had the wrong letter.'

'Indeed he did, but he didn't know that then.'

'But I never told him he'd stolen the wrong one.'

Beniamino shook his head. 'You didn't need to. You relaxed after a while, so we all knew that whatever the crisis was that led to the ship being searched, it had died down. Now, if you're Hendriks, that must give you a bad feeling. Perhaps he opened the letter then; at any event he must have realised by the time you docked that he did not have the right missive.'

'So I was wrong to suspect Velders? I carefully avoided walking through any narrow alleys with him for fear that he would finish off the job he had started.'

'No, Velders came ashore with you to ensure your safety. You see, if he knew he had not stolen your letter it wouldn't be too difficult for him to guess who might have done. But he could hardly accuse his own deputy without some hard evidence, so the best he could do was see that you came to no harm. And I was grateful, because as a mere seaman I couldn't just leave the ship whenever I wanted, so seeing him leave with you was a relief to me.'

'So, if Velders was protecting me, why did he desert me at the water pump?'

'Yes, that puzzled me for a while, but Hendriks explained it a couple of days ago when we were having a little talk below decks.'

'A little talk?'

Beniamino shrugged. 'I posed a few questions, and he answered them. Eventually.'

My mind reverted to those tools with which Beniamino had attended to my cut head. 'When you attended to my cut, those actually were torture instruments, weren't they?'

'They may have been,' Beniamino conceded. 'Surgical instruments and torture instruments are very similar. It's all in how you wield them.'

'Those tweezers you used to remove the splinter from my head — they were the same ones you used to pull fingernails out, weren't they?'

Beniamino lengthened his stride. 'Oh, Master, do you really want to know?'

I caught up with him as we crested a hill. Before us I could see a sleepy seaport waking to greet the day.

'Lyme Regis,' said Beniamino.

'Is this our destination?'

For answer, Beniamino pointed out to sea. 'There's the *Nieuwpoort.*'

'That's a relief. I thought I might never see it again.'

'Don't relax your vigilance. We need to be sure that the King's agents haven't set a trap for us when we try to rejoin it.'

'Why would they do that?'

Beniamino shook his head. 'You didn't see the English ship following us when we left London?'

'English ship? No.'

'You need to improve your observation if you're going to make a career of this, Mercurius.'

I was highly peeved to hear this. 'For your information,' I snapped, 'the only career I want is that of a moral philosophy lecturer who divides his time between the University library and Steen's inn.'

My rescuer smiled that strange, slightly twisted smile of his. 'You shouldn't be so good at it, then.'

'Believe me, I've tried very hard to fail.'

'No, you haven't. You don't have it in you.'

He was right. My stupid pride would not allow me to deliberately fail, though I had done so this time.

'You never explained why Velders left me at the water pump,' I said.

'Because he saw Hendriks. Why traipse around London in your company when he could stay close by the threat? So he left you to follow Hendriks.'

'And Hendriks saw him too?'

'Yes, and realised that to escape discovery he would have to ensure that Velders could not tell his tale. He launched a murderous attack but London is a busy city. When he heard someone coming he was obliged to break off his assault and flee. Now, I suggest we continue this discussion later and concentrate on finding a small boat.'

'By finding, you mean stealing.'

'I don't intend to deprive anyone permanently of their boat, Mercurius. We will cast it loose when we are done with it. Unless, of course, your scruples require you to row back and swim out to the ship?'

'I can't swim.'

Beniamino's jaw dropped. 'You're a Dutchman and you can't swim?'

'I can manage a few strokes. But that ship is a long way out to sea.'

'Well, I hope you can row a boat,' said Beniamino.

I had not tried for years, but how hard could it be, I wondered?

CHAPTER NINETEEN

'And stroke, and stroke, and stroke...!' ordered Beniamino.

'I'm trying,' I complained, 'and your shouting at me isn't helping.'

'I am not shouting. I am trying to keep us in rhythm so that we start going forward rather than spinning aimlessly.'

Rowing a boat turned out to be harder than I had remembered. For some reason moving both arms at once seemed remarkably difficult, and since my right arm is stronger than my left we seemed to be pursuing a curved path. This was understandable because Beniamino's right arm was probably stronger than his left too; and frankly I am not sure how good he was at steering anyway.

It soon became clear that unless we changed course we were going to miss the *Nieuwpoort* by some distance so Beniamino ordered me to stop rowing on the left.

'No, Mercurius, the left of the boat, which means your right hand.'

'This is all very difficult. Can't you keep to simple instructions such as a landsman might understand?'

'Very well. Stop rowing with your right hand so the pointy end swings to the left.'

'That's better. I can follow that.'

I am fairly certain that the *Nieuwpoort* was steering away from us, because even after we had been rowing for fifteen minutes we seemed to be little nearer.

'We're rowing against the tide,' Beniamino explained. 'But the tide will be turning soon.'

I was too breathless to pick up the conversation. I do not wish to be thought to be a complainer, but I was cold, still hungry, wet through, tired and annoyed with myself for so completely misunderstanding what had happened in London. How could I have been such a dunderhead? I had convinced myself that Velders must be the guilty party and that Hendriks was assisting me, and now I tried to think why I had gone wrong.

I had allowed myself to believe that only Velders and I knew the contents of the Stadhouder's letter, which had proved to be incorrect. I had also not expected anyone on the *Nieuwpoort* to be opposed to the Stadhouder's policy, insofar as any of us actually knew what his policy really was, because I would not have put it past him to have me deliver bogus plans to deceive the English when actually he had some other stratagem in mind. I placed my trust in the honesty of Princess Mary, who would, I believed, have dealt fairly with me; and since she had reassured me that her husband had no intention of assisting the Duke of Monmouth I was disposed to take her at her word. This generosity of spirit towards a Stuart woman did not, incidentally, extend to her sister, Princess Anne, who could be a scheming little madam; still, that is a story for another day.

My blood ran cold to think that while Velders was lying in the hospital I had trusted Hendriks completely. I had even thought of giving him the letter to keep in a place of safety. 'If you knew all this,' I asked Beniamino, 'why didn't you warn me?'

Beniamino smiled. 'I thought if an uneducated nincompoop like me knew what was going on, surely a university man would do so.'

That smarted.

'Besides which,' Beniamino continued, 'I didn't know it then. You forget that I was confined to the ship; how then should I have discovered this?'

'But you did discover it. So how?'

'Can we shut up and just row? I will explain everything when we are safely on the ship.'

The quicker I row the sooner we will be there and the faster I shall find out what has been taking place under my nose, I thought, so I redoubled my efforts and gave the oars a mighty pull.

Unfortunately I lost control of the left oar which bounced out of the little cup that cradled it and dropped into the sea. 'It wasn't my fault,' I exclaimed automatically.

'Well, who else's could it be?' sighed Beniamino, who stopped rowing.

'Don't give up,' I counselled. 'We can use one oar each.'

'We could,' conceded Beniamino. 'Alternatively you could reach over the side and grab the oar now that it has floated back to the surface. No, on second thoughts, you'd better not lean over the side. Swap places and I'll get it. And don't row while I'm leaning over.'

Half an hour later we drew alongside the *Nieuwpoort* and the men dropped a net over the side for us to clamber aboard.

'Don't look down,' said Beniamino. 'And make sure that three of your four limbs are always in contact with the net.'

If ever advice was unnecessary, that was. 'Don't worry,' I told him. 'I will.'

A couple of sailors reached down to lift me over the side. I was so thrilled to be on the ship that I gave serious thought to kissing the deck until I saw the state of the sailors' bare feet.

'Welcome aboard, Master,' called Wilkens from the little raised deck at the back of the ship. [No, Van der Meer, I have not made it my business to find out what it is called. My readers will understand.] 'We feared we might not see you again.'

'I feared that too,' I admitted. 'I was close to being hanged.'

'No, not then,' Wilkens said. 'When you were about to lean over to fetch the oar.'

Young men can be so impolite. However, I have been schooled by undergraduates and rose above his taunting.

Wilkens must have recognised that he had gone too far, for he immediately addressed the crew. 'Let us give thanks to God for the safe return of the Master. Will you lead us, Master?'

The men dropped to their knees without awaiting a reply, so I mumbled a few words, then managed to frame a more coherent prayer of thanks for my deliverance. All the while Beniamino leaned against a mast with an amused look on his face, so I included him in my prayers, thanking God for sending him as His agent to save His poor servant.

The sailors returned to their posts and Beniamino clapped a hand on my shoulder.

'I am touched, Master.'

'I meant it. God sent you to save me.'

Beniamino shook his head. 'No, Master, the Stadhouder sent me. And the Stadhouder is not God.' He walked towards the cabins, then paused at the doorway. 'But I don't think I want to be the one who tells him that.'

The next time I saw Beniamino he had shaved off his beard and dressed his hair. I had left some of my belongings on the ship so at least I had a clean shirt to wear. The cook made me a plate of bacon and beans that did much to restore me. It was so good to taste authentic Dutch cooking again. I had a brief mental image of Mechtild pausing in her work to gaze out of the window to see if I was returning; nonsense, of course, because the kitchen windows face away from the canal, but a potent reminder of home none the less. I have no family now. Mechtild is like an aunt to me, which I suppose makes Albrecht my uncle. Well, so be it. They are good people, even if one of them is an atrocious cook.

Beniamino sat opposite me and accepted a similar plate. 'Are you recovered now, Master?' he asked.

'It will take a little while. I am not accustomed to peril.'

Needless to say, one cannot be a member of a Faculty of Theology without occasionally being subjected to robust treatment by opponents. I remember a symposium on the desirability or otherwise of infant baptism that became very heated and in which a number of very strong words were used, including a couple I had to look up when I returned to my room. [You will have to guess, Van der Meer. I cannot repeat them.]

Nevertheless, all this climbing, running, paddling and rowing had left me feeling exhausted. It is possible that the strain of knowing what would happen if we were caught played some part in this though, strangely, I somehow had confidence in Beniamino's resourcefulness to extricate us from such danger.

'Beniamino, if the Mayor's men had caught up with us, what would you have done?'

Beniamino paused, his spoon hovering halfway to his mouth. 'I don't know. They didn't, so I didn't have to think about it.'

'But — humour me — what if they had?'

Beniamino rested his spoon on his plate, wiped his mouth and stared at the ceiling for a short while as if this aided cogitation. 'Well, let us look at this logically, as I imagine a university lecturer would want to do.'

'Certainly.' I was on very familiar ground here.

'If they had caught us,' Beniamino began, 'they would not have been as interested in me as in you. I have been trained to withstand ill-treatment and they would not have got much out of me. You, on the other hand, would have suffered terribly at the hands of any torturer.'

I doubted that. Shown the instruments of torture I would at once have volunteered all the information I possessed on any subject that interested them; but I wasn't going to tell Beniamino that.

'Even though you would probably squeal all you knew right at the outset, they would continue to torment you to set an example to any other prisoner who might be minded to escape. Think of Guy Fawkes, so enfeebled by his torture that he was scarce able to climb the ladder to the gallows. That is how thorough the English can be.'

I had not heard of this man Fawkes, but I have since discovered that he conceived a scheme for removing the great men of England by creating a mighty explosion under the Parliament House in the time of King James' grandfather, also called James.

'And since the purpose of your mission appeared to them to be to remove King James from the throne, you could expect very similar treatment. I like you, Mercurius. I could not allow that to happen to you.'

I was deeply touched. My confidence in Beniamino was not misplaced.

'Therefore I would have slit your throat before they arrested us.'

I felt my hand caressing my neck involuntarily. I suppose his proposed action would have been the merciful thing to do, but I cannot say that I was entirely comfortable with the idea.

'Wouldn't the Stadhouder have been cross if you did that?' I asked.

'An interesting question. I think he would have viewed it as a necessary sacrifice. Of course, he would have been sad for a moment or two. He is a pious man and might well have said a prayer commending you. Then someone would have reminded him that it was dinner-time or he had a new horse to break in and he would have forgotten us both.'

I wish he would forget me, I thought. *It would be lovely to be left in peace in the library for a while. Or possibly forever.*

Beniamino finished his plate and pushed it away with a satisfied belch. 'You asked me how I uncovered what had happened, Master. It is very simple. Hendriks told me.'

'He told you?'

'I encouraged him, of course.'

I had no doubt what that meant. I had seen Beniamino at work. Hendriks was probably missing a finger or two by now. I did not need to know the details.

'Naturally, I did not have all the tools I would have wanted. Fire on a wooden ship is discouraged, so Wilkens asked me not to use a hot poker. But the carpenter lent me a rasp and I found that rubbing Hendriks' privities with it and then splashing them with salt water was a great tongue-loosener.'

I could believe that.

'And the sailors had a number of fishing hooks that they were prepared to lend me.'

I felt faint. I could almost have felt some sympathy for Hendriks had I not recalled what he had done to poor Velders; besides which, he had made me look stupid, and I felt that insult very keenly. 'So what did Hendriks tell you?'

'Simply that he had realised that he had the wrong letter, and reasoned that you must know that too, because you were less frantic than you had been when the loss of the Duke's plans became known. Therefore, he thought, you would not risk the same thing happening again, and would keep the letter about your person. He followed you with the intention of waylaying you somewhere and stealing the letter. He would have hit you from behind so that, if you saw him, he could claim that he had frightened off an assailant.'

I might have fallen for that, given my presuppositions that Velders was the guilty party.

'Then,' Beniamino continued, 'he trailed you to the ambassador's house. He thought that you were going to leave the letter there for safekeeping, so when you left, he remained, trying to plot his next move. But seeing the ambassador returning, he realised that you could not have met him, and surely you would not entrust so important a letter to a maid. Thus emboldened, he chased after you with a view to intercepting you before you reached the ship.'

'And where was Velders?'

'Velders had seen Hendriks and was looking for him. Hendriks did not see him for a while, and he did not know where Velders had been in the meantime, but he saw him again as he neared the river, and attacked him from behind. He feared that Velders would denounce him to you. Hendriks, you see, is a fanatical Protestant. He detests Catholics and wishes nothing more than that England should be firmly in the Protestant camp. That is why he desires to further the cause of the Duke of Monmouth against King James. He guessed that what William gave you could not be bogus plans, or they would not serve their purpose. The King would move his troops to the wrong place. They must be Monmouth's true invasion plans.'

'It was the Stadhouder's idea that if the King knew where Monmouth was heading he could put on a display of force that would discourage futile bloodshed and persuade Monmouth to abandon his invasion.'

Beniamino chuckled. 'You know Monmouth is selling all his worldly goods to finance his campaign? How could he turn back? He has nothing to return to. All his hopes rest on this adventure, and he will essay it, though he be outnumbered six to one.'

'You think so?'

'I know so. How do you think the Stadhouder got hold of the plans?'

The awful realisation struck me like a spade to the head. 'You?'

'I have been in Monmouth's camp for some time. Disguised as a Prussian mercenary, of course.'

Such were his powers of disguise that I would not have been surprised to hear that he had been masquerading as a horse.

'So the Duke may be on his way to invade England even as we speak?'

'I doubt it, for two reasons. First, because the English weather is uncertain. Bad weather favours the defenders, so he will probably wait until May or June. Second, I doubt it because of what Hendriks did.'

'What did Hendriks do?'

'Why do you think the *Nieuwpoort* was not at the quay in Exeter as arranged?'

I had not given this any thought. 'Presumably because it proved too difficult to navigate it upriver from Topsham.'

'Nearly. The difficulty of navigation is relevant, but not in the way you think. The Duke's plans call for him to land his soldiers in Exeter and then follow the high road towards

London. Exeter is not as well garrisoned as it might be, but the Duke's forces are not much superior in number. However, the narrowness of the river and the need for a high tide mean that the ships would have to approach in single file, land their troops, and then move to allow more to disembark. Meanwhile the defenders could pick off each successive shipload as soon as they landed. From the military point of view, invading through Exeter makes no sense, and Hendriks could see that. So he took the ship off in search of a better landing ground, which is why we came to Lyme Regis. There is a large bay, plenty of beaches to land on and from there Monmouth can march north-east to Yeovil and find the high road, leaving the garrison at Exeter behind him.'

'But how did you wrest control of the ship from him?'

'I had to think fast, because Hendriks was minded to look for an even better port, which would have taken him yet further east and left you stranded without hope of deliverance. I can walk thirty miles; any further would have left me unable to help. But I spoke to the crew below decks and told them the truth about what Hendriks had done. Velders was a popular captain. And when I embellished the story a little by telling them that Hendriks aimed to cause another war between England and our country, they were ready to help me overpower him.'

I was impressed. Beniamino must be quite an orator.

'Then I played my trump card,' he continued. 'I told them you would give them a lot of money when we returned.'

I quaked. 'I don't have a lot of money.'

'Master,' Beniamino smiled, 'what you have seems like a lot of money to them. And I'm sure we can persuade the Stadhouder to spare a few guilders when we get back to Hellevoetsluis.'

I would not have been optimistic about that. William was a notorious tightwad at the best of times, when you had some advantage over him; the chances of getting cash from him when you had already rendered him the service seemed slight to me. But maybe Beniamino planned to use those diabolical tools of his to persuade the Stadhouder?

I took a gulp of ale and tried to parcel together all the information Beniamino had given me. I had been fortunate indeed to make my way back to the ship; I could not have done it without him. He had succeeded where I had failed miserably. 'I suppose,' I said, 'that now the Duke will follow his original plan, land at Exeter and innocent men will be slaughtered.'

'Not necessarily,' Beniamino replied.

'How do you mean?'

Beniamino leaned forward and lowered his voice. 'How shall it profit our master if King James has an easy victory? Of course, James must win, or Monmouth will seize the throne and William and Mary will lose it. But William would really prefer the King and the Duke to fight each other to the point of exhaustion. He would like to see whether all the lords of England come to their King's aid, or whether some choose to be diplomatically away from home when the summons comes. This could be a really good time for some lords to visit their farthest estates for a prolonged holiday. Some are even thinking of visiting their in-laws.'

I do not have in-laws, but I understand that many men try hard to have little contact with their wives' family once they have the dowry in hand.

'Therefore,' continued Beniamino, 'refining the Duke's plan so that he lands at Lyme Regis gives him a better chance of being a real nuisance without risking him actually winning.'

'Is King James a good general?'

'No, but he has advisers who are. Unless the men of the western counties declare for the Duke he will not raise the armies he needs for victory. And I doubt they will. They have little interest in what happens outside their own counties and some affection for the King's late father.'

'So how will you convey this information to the Duke? You can't let Hendriks report back.'

'No, but I might be able to return to his camp as the Prussian he knows. I shall have Hendriks' written report to give him.'

'Will Hendriks write one?'

'Maybe. Maybe not. But I doubt that the Duke knows Hendriks' handwriting. We just have to make sure that Hendriks doesn't land in the United Provinces to give any other account.'

'You mean to leave him somewhere else?'

'I mean to throw him overboard with a large weight attached to him. We cannot take him home.'

'That would be murder. He ought to have a proper trial.'

'If he does, the Duke will hear of it and begin to doubt the report that I have given him.'

I could see the quandary we were in, but executing a man in cold blood did not sit well with me. Although it went against the grain, I had to think of a way to save Hendriks.

CHAPTER TWENTY

It was long after dark, but sleep eluded me. Despite my tiredness, the ship's motion disturbed me, added to which my brain refused to rest.

I was troubled by the fate of Hendriks who was in his cabin, shackled to his bed with Beniamino keeping him company to ensure that he did not escape. I had instinctively rejected Beniamino's plan to throw Hendriks overboard as barbaric, but, viewed from another angle, was there really any difference between taking him home to be hanged and drowning him now? A few extra days of life, certainly, but would they be a blessing if filled with apprehension of what was to come?

After all, the man was a murderer. Ah, but he wasn't, because — so far as I knew — Velders was not dead. He had been robbed of all that made life worthwhile, but he was still breathing. Whatever the law was on the matter, from a moral standpoint I could see little distinction between killing someone and rendering them permanently incapable. I would have to discuss that with colleagues to collect their views before pronouncing definitively, but if that were right, then Hendriks should not escape hanging on the technicality that he was not proficient as a murderer.

But then, what if we executed Hendriks and after a period Velders should recover? It was not unknown for men at death's door to suddenly return to health, albeit with some lasting damage. When I was a boy and we went to the market people would point out Old Piet to me, who, many years before, had somehow managed to get hit on the head by a windmill's sail and was unconscious for two weeks so that his funeral was being planned when, to everyone's surprise, he sat up and asked for a cup of ale. My grandfather said it was difficult to tell if his wits had been impaired by his accident because Old Piet was not over-endowed with intelligence before the incident, and, as my grandmother noted, if Old Piet had any brains he would not have leaned out of a windmill in the first place.

On the other hand — and when you are a moral philosopher there is always something "on the other hand" — if word reached the Duke of Monmouth that Hendriks was a prisoner he might well suspect that he had been betrayed, and the person at whom he would point the finger would be his cousin William. The fact that he would be right in doing so was beside the point, or at least that is what William would say, because William would believe that his plan was flawless. He always did.

These thoughts oppressed me. I never liked capital punishment, nor do I now. We make it a ghastly spectacle so as to deter others from following the same path, yet it seems to make no difference. The hardened criminal believes that he will not be caught, so the penalty is irrelevant; and others act impulsively with no thought as to the consequences, moved by some powerful passion of the moment. I do not doubt that some men are wicked enough to merit death, but I leave that in the hands of God, who is surely able to smite those who need a good smiting, and forbear when He wishes to show mercy; I cannot overlook that if we get what we deserve from God at the Last Judgment, we are all in big trouble.

It may seem strange to discuss the fate of Hendriks as a logical puzzle, but by doing so I began to see a course of action. The difficulty would arise if the Duke ever discovered that Hendriks had been discovered and imprisoned. However, sometime in the next two to three months the Duke would leave our lands to make his bid for the English throne. If he succeeded he would not care that Hendriks was incarcerated, and if he failed it was certain that King James would soon have him killed. Seen in that light, all I had to do was devise some means of keeping Hendriks out of sight for a little while until the Duke had left. Naturally, I would also have to ensure that the crew of the *Nieuwpoort* did not give the game away, but I could probably do that with money.

I shaved and had some breakfast before climbing up on deck to see if I could see the Low Countries yet, and found the ship's crew in a state of some excitement.

'What's happening?' I asked Wilkens.

'Look behind you,' he replied.

I looked but all I could see was sea. Admittedly there was quite a lot of it, but I could not imagine that would cause such consternation in sailors. 'What am I looking for?' I enquired.

'There!' Wilkens pointed into the distance, but to no avail. I could not see anything worth looking at. 'Do you not see the ship, Master?'

Now that he mentioned it, there was a small smudge in the distance, but I could not have discerned it as a ship.

'How far away is it?'

'Not far enough. It's an English man-o'-war, Master, and it seems to be chasing us.'

The *Nieuwpoort* had some arms, but since it was not intended to be a threat to the English it was not a warship. However, I understood that it was quick. 'Isn't the *Nieuwpoort* faster than any man-o'-war?'

'Yes, in comparable winds. But soon we will be passing the south-east corner of England and heading out into open sea. It is possible we shall meet with northerly winds that will drive us towards France and allow the English to catch up.'

I think that I have mentioned that my brother Laurentius died in a sea-battle against the English near a place called Lowestoft. I had no wish to make this a family habit. Very occasionally, when I am in a maudlin humour, I contemplate the circumstances of my death. I usually picture a scene in which I am propped up by large, fluffy pillows in my own familiar bed, well-stricken in years, in possession of my faculties as I dictate my final wishes for the disbursement of my effects. [Van der Meer has just asked if he is taking the dictation. I cannot say. My attention is entirely on my own part in this drama.]

Somehow I find that vision comforting, and the notion that I might die anywhere else is disquieting. On this particular day thirty-six years ago I faced the prospect of a watery grave, and I cannot say that I approached it with equanimity, so much so that I urged the sailors to raise more sail and was perfectly prepared to paddle a bit if they had an oar long enough.

Wilkens was displaying a capacity for command remarkable in so young a man. He looked up to the top of one of the masts. Following his gaze I could see a poor sailor who had been stationed there.

'What news?' Wilkens yelled.

'She's coming across towards the north,' came the reply.

'The captain is probably trying to get into calmer water,' Wilkens told me. 'I can see no other reason to drift towards the coast.'

'Why would he be pursuing us anyway?' I asked in genuine perplexity.

'You,' said Beniamino, who had sneaked up silently behind me. I wished he would not do that. I found it very unnerving.

'Me?'

'You're a fugitive, and they must have realised a Dutchman is likely to be on board a Dutch ship that left hurriedly. A fast horse will outrun a ship, so even with our head start they would be able to send out a ship from the Solent to try to intercept us. Fortunately the wind has been favourable thus far. But it is not impossible that another horseman is riding for Dover to repeat the exercise.'

A tense hour passed, but then the lookout announced that the pursuer had given up and was heading into port. I breathed a sigh of relief.

'Not so quick, Master,' Beniamino said. 'He may have given up believing that another pursuer lies in wait for us.'

So it proved. As we neared Dover we could see an English ship idly drifting while awaiting our arrival. The sea is narrow there, but not so narrow that we could not slip past, which is what Wilkens determined to do.

'She's a big ship,' Beniamino remarked.

'Big and tall,' Wilkens replied, 'and therefore likely not to be as manoeuvrable as this beauty.'

I cannot quite explain how Wilkens did what he did next, but he set a course that took the *Nieuwpoort* between the English ship and the coast. The English turned their ship around to return landwards, and when they were fully turned he swung our ship to the right as if to sneak past on the French side. The English were obliged to turn again.

'Ready the guns!' he ordered.

The sailors rushed to obey. The guns were quite small, I thought, though what does a cleric know about ordnance?

Wilkens made to swerve once again. The English followed suit, as if anticipating his move, but he straightened his course once more.

'One of us needs to go down to the deck to give the order to fire at the right time,' he said.

For a horrible moment I thought he was expecting me to volunteer, until I realised that his remark was addressed to Beniamino.

'You steer, and I'll fire,' said the torture master.

'Maximum elevation to give the longest range,' Wilkens ordered. 'We'll probably only get a couple of volleys off but it may be enough.'

Beniamino nodded, and made his way down. If there were going to be cannonballs flying around I really wanted to be somewhere less exposed, ideally a tavern on dry land, but I could see nowhere safe to hide and while going below was an option, then I would not know what was taking place above me. I decided the best thing I could do would be to crouch a little so as to present a smaller target.

The English were still turning to return to us when Beniamino gave the order to fire. Both shots missed the ship, but not by as much as I had expected, and the English ship slowed momentarily as if assessing the odds of being hit. It was at this point that even a landlubber like myself could see Wilkens' plan. We could fire at them from the left side of our ship, but since they were head on to us they could not train their guns on us. The English captain tried to swing his ship sideways on to us and we braced ourselves for the coming salvo, but when the shots were fired they dropped short, at which I sighed with relief.

'Don't be too optimistic, Master,' Wilkens told me. 'They'll correct before their next shot which will be a lot closer. If you know any good prayers, now is the time to say them.'

Whether my prayers were objectively good, I cannot say; they were certainly heartfelt. I thought Wilkens might veer to the right to increase the distance between us and the English, but he did not.

'There's no point, Master. I just lengthen our voyage if I do that and the English will close on us anyway.'

Instead he turned slightly to the left and we had the satisfaction that the next cannonball passed behind us. The one after that flew over us, which Wilkens viewed with a satisfaction that I did not quite share.

I had completely lost track of time, but as I looked behind us I saw the most welcome sight. 'The sun is setting,' I remarked.

Wilkens glanced behind him. 'And it is starting to rain, God be praised. I knew rain could never be far away in England.'

Being a pedant, I was obliged to observe that we were not in England.

'No, Master, but nonetheless the English weather is welcome. It will reduce visibility, and soon it will be dark and we should be able to slip away.'

The next cannonball came far too close for my liking, but Wilkens appeared unperturbed. Raising his spyglass to his eye he smiled.

'They're lowering sail to steady the ship. The next volley will determine our fate.'

If there is one thing I know how to do it is to pray, so I dropped to my knees and did some of the fastest praying I have ever done in my life. It was not decorous but it was comprehensive. I brought to mind the Psalm which says: *They that go down to the sea in ships, doing business in the great waters: These have seen the works of the Lord, and his wonders in the deep. He said the word, and there arose a storm of wind: and the waves thereof were lifted up.*

Now would be a really good time to raise a storm of wind, I prayed; I will not claim that it happened immediately but very soon afterwards the wind got up and we accelerated away just as cannonballs landed a little behind us. The *Nieuwpoort* was certainly built for speed, and with a good wind we were able to put the English well to our rear.

Beniamino joined us. 'I don't think you'll be welcome in London again for a while, Master,' he said.

'I don't think I care,' I answered him.

This meant, of course, that I could not return to see Velders once more and apologise to him for suspecting him; which reminded me that Hendriks was still in the cabin below. I wanted to have a few words with him, if Beniamino would permit it.

'Be my guest. He was rather surly when I spoke to him earlier.'

'Indeed?'

'Yes. I told him that if he tried to escape I would nail his hands to the beams, which he took umbrage at, but it is as well to be plain about these things.'

I cringed. I had no doubt that Beniamino was in earnest, though why Hendriks would attempt to escape I could not say, since even the strongest swimmer had little chance of reaching land in these icy waters.

'If you don't object,' Beniamino added, 'I think I'll come with you. He may have ideas about taking you hostage to barter for his freedom.'

That had not occurred to me, so I readily assented, and together we descended to the cabin where our criminal was stowed. Beniamino opened the door, and a pitiful sight greeted me.

Hendriks' face was bruised and some of his teeth were missing. He cradled his left hand in his right, and hurried to withdraw his chained legs and roll into a ball as if anticipating a further beating. 'Pity!' he cried. 'Have pity!'

Beniamino was unmoved. 'What pity have you earned?' he asked sternly, and drew a truncheon from his belt.

'Mercy! No more, I beg!'

'Behave yourself and answer the Master's questions, and you'll be used well. If not, you know what lies in store.'

Hendriks nodded.

I looked for somewhere to sit, and perched on the lid of a chest. 'You know the fate that awaits you?' I began.

'I shall hang, or worse. But I shall die.'

'And you know that you deserve it?'

'I was serving a just cause. Surely you of all people want to see a Protestant England and popery banished thence?'

That was a sore point, but I could not let him know that. 'I do not want to see a man like Velders clubbed down and bludgeoned near to death.'

Hendriks shuddered. 'If I could have avoided it I would have done, but he knew what I was about. Once he knew that I was the Duke's man, I was bound for hanging whatever I did, if not for murder then for acting against the Stadhouder.'

I turned this over in my mind a few times. 'You are the Duke of Monmouth's man?'

'I have sworn to support him.'

I had spent enough time in William's company to know what his reaction to these tidings would be. He had been so busy plotting against the Duke that it had not occurred to him that the Duke might have agents watching what William was doing; and if Hendriks was one such, who knew how many more there might be?

'Do you know what the Stadhouder sent me to England to achieve?' I asked.

'You were to betray the Duke by handing over his plans.'

'No — well, yes, but I didn't know that they were genuine. I thought they were plans forged by the Stadhouder. Anyway, the point was the same either way; by giving the information to King James he would be able to face down Monmouth's army and, we hoped, bloodshed would be averted when the Duke saw the futility of his invasion. The Stadhouder does not want the Duke defeated; he wants there to be no battle.'

Hendriks' face creased into a wry smile. 'Then he will be disappointed, for the Duke will hazard all on one roll of the dice. He is just awaiting my report suggesting a suitable landing-place.'

Beniamino seemed to know what I was thinking. 'Master, this is a very bad idea...' he began.

'Maybe. But if it fails then I get to pass my days in a library with no further calls on my services, and that suits me very well.'

'I am not accustomed to failure,' he growled.

'Neither success nor failure is certain,' I answered him. 'All we are doing is letting things play out as they will.' I addressed Hendriks again. 'You say the Duke will invade whatever we do?'

'I am certain of it.'

'If he does there will be great bloodshed, I do not think many Englishmen will take up arms against their King again.'

'The Duke is a man of honour. Whatever befalls him, he will try his hand.'

'Since I believe that he will fail, I will make you a bargain. Write your report, but leave it unsealed so that we may read it. My colleague here will see that it is delivered. When we reach land you will be secretly taken ashore and imprisoned there until the Duke has left. Then I will conduct you to the Stadhouder and he will decide your fate. I will recommend mercy in exchange for your co-operation but you must realise that I cannot bind the Stadhouder.'

'My report will not be altered or substituted?'

Beniamino gripped Hendriks' hands and squeezed, causing the prisoner to yelp with pain. 'I do not think that your bargaining position is very strong,' Beniamino hissed. 'I would accept the deal if I were you. It is far more generous than any I would offer.'

'If you hurt my hands I will not be able to write,' whimpered Hendriks.

Beniamino let him go. I could see that both thumbs were swollen, presumably the result of his persuasive methods.

'The Duke will expect me to report in person,' Hendriks said.

'Sadly you died at sea of a fever,' I told him. 'That explains the shaky handwriting. But before you died you entrusted your report to me and I, being innocent of its contents, gave it to a certain Prussian officer I know.'

'If I am thought dead I cannot support the Duke's cause, and I would be forsworn,' he pointed out.

'Which is better?' I asked him. 'To be thought dead, or actually to be dead? I know which I would prefer.'

Hendriks addressed Beniamino. 'If you are a barber, pray dress my hands so that I can hold a quill.'

To my surprise Beniamino fetched water and bandages, and attended to Hendriks' needs with every sentiment of concern. He rubbed the hands gently with a salve and dressed them with strips of linen.

'Now, Lieutenant Hendriks,' he said. 'Prevaricate no more. Write your report, and write it as you would give it to your master in person. The voyage is not over yet, and there is plenty of sea between here and Hellevoetsluis in which to throw you if you displease me.'

CHAPTER TWENTY-ONE

Hendriks' report was brief but informative. He said that he had viewed the port at Exeter and it was wholly unsuited to landing the Duke's troops. They could disembark at Topsham, but then they would have over an hour's march into Exeter during which the defenders would have noticed that they were coming. On his own initiative he had reconnoitred further east and had found an admirable landing place at Lyme Regis. He did not believe that it was necessary to capture Exeter; the troops there were too few to threaten the Duke's rear and landing at Lyme Regis would put him a day's march nearer to London.

Beniamino persisted in his belief that this was not a good idea. 'I could put him to death very suddenly,' he insisted. 'A garrotte is good. He would hardly feel a thing.'

'Apart from not being able to breathe,' I said.

'Well, obviously.'

We leaned on the rail and gazed out to sea, standing side by side.

'What are your plans?' I asked.

'We'll get him ashore as part of your half-baked plan, I'll report to the Stadhouder and then resume my Prussian persona to infiltrate the Duke's camp.'

I felt a sudden pang of concern for this man who had now saved me twice. 'If he does invade, will you be with him?'

Beniamino grimaced. 'If I can avoid it, I will. If I'm on any ship other than his, I can probably desert. But if he depends on me as much as he has hitherto, I may be at his side. In which event, I will fight for him as if my life depended on it, because it probably will.'

'Do you have much experience of battle?'

'Too much.' He bowed his head and mumbled some further words. 'The first day was too much.'

We stood in companionable silence a while. The weather was good, and the wind was pushing us homeward. What more could I want?

There was one obvious desideratum. I needed an explanation for William as to how I had completely misunderstood the attack on Velders and failed to divine that Hendriks was working for the Duke. Against that, I thought I deserved an explanation for sending me on a mission that was apparently sufficiently hazardous for me to need a clandestine bodyguard. William would probably attempt to bluster his way out of that one, telling me he had not apprehended real danger and that Beniamino was just a safeguard, but given the violence to which Hendriks had been prepared to resort the stakes were higher than William had revealed to me.

Just before dusk we had our first sight of land, at which I rejoiced greatly. Unfortunately, it was the wrong bit of land. It transpired that this was Flanders, and we had some way to go before reaching our own country. We passed the mouths of several rivers before Wilkens was satisfied that we were in the right place and turned the ship towards its home port. I have no idea how sailors tell one river mouth from another, or recognise ports, but somehow Wilkens found Hellevoetsluis and shortly after breakfast we drew up alongside our berth and I was able to walk down the gangplank and feel the good honest earth of the United Provinces beneath my feet, something which I had thought I would never feel again just a few days earlier.

I remained there while the crew did whatever a crew does when a ship reaches its destination. There were ropes to stow away, sails to furl, and so on, then the men were allowed to muster to receive their pay. On the assumption that William would reimburse me, something that I must have been remarkably bold to assume, I augmented their money with a little extra in exchange for their silence about what they had seen. Fortunately with Velders and Hendriks receiving no pay there was some extra in the kitty to share between the ordinary sailors.

After a little while a party of sailors approached me and deposited my trunk and a barrel beside me.

'Your luggage, Master,' said one.

'There must be some mistake,' I replied. 'The trunk is mine, certainly, but the barrel…'

'…is yours also,' interrupted Beniamino, giving me a hard stare.

'If you say so,' I stuttered, altogether unsure what he was driving at.

The sailors were sent by Beniamino to see about hiring a horse and cart, and when they were out of earshot he explained. 'The barrel contains your extra luggage. It was all we had.'

'Extra luggage?'

Beniamino sighed and prised the bung out of the barrel before inviting me to look inside. Hendriks was trussed up and gagged. 'It's probably a good idea if you don't leave the bung in once you're on the cart or he may suffocate,' said Beniamino.

'Aren't you coming with me?'

'I need to find out where the Duke of Monmouth is first.'

'Nobody will know that better than William.'

'How will he know when I'm not in the Duke's camp to tell him?'

He had a point.

'Princess Mary told me his fleet was at Texel.'

Beniamino looked surprised that I should remember this. 'Is it indeed? Then the chances are that he will be north rather than south of here. All right, Master; I will come with you to The Hague and report to the Stadhouder. But if your barrel falls off the cart and rolls away, or your idiotic scheme comes apart in any other way, don't expect my help.'

As you may imagine, hearing my wonderfully cunning plan described in this fashion cast something of a chill over our conversation for the first part of the journey, at least as far as the ferry that took us across to Maasluis. There we had some animated discussion with the ferryman who judged our horse and cart, the trunk and the barrel to be too heavy a load for one trip and wanted to leave the luggage behind for a second crossing, presumably with one of us to guard it, which would have slowed our journey considerably, but Beniamino persuaded him to try on the understanding that if we began to sink he would kick the barrel over the side. The contents of the barrel became rather agitated on hearing this and Beniamino was obliged to lean on it to ensure that it did not rock.

Barely nine hours after we left Hellevoetsluis we reached The Hague and made our way to the gates of the Binnenhof.

'Tradesmen round the back,' barked the guard.

'We are not tradesmen,' Beniamino replied, 'and smarten yourself up when you speak to an officer or I'll have you flogged.'

'Yes, sir,' replied the hapless guard, who clearly recognised the tone of command.

'Is the Stadhouder in the Palace?'

'No, sir. He's at his other place at Apeldoorn.'

This was bad news. I did not fancy another day on the cart, particularly in the company of one whose mood was darkening by the minute.

'Then we will send to him to tell him we are here. Ask the Captain of the Guard to send us a fast horseman.'

'Pardon me, sir,' gulped the guard, 'but on what authority…'

'On this authority,' Beniamino answered, producing a dagger with lightning rapidity and gripping the poor man's throat with the other hand.

I felt the need to intervene. 'Is Secretary Bouwman here?'

'Oh, yes, sir. The Stadhouder is expecting to return tomorrow.'

'Excellent. If we may see mijnheer Bouwman I think we need not keep you from your duties any longer.'

The grateful guard hurried to fetch the Stadhouder's Secretary, who greeted us cordially and invited us to his office where he would arrange for wine and supper for us. He was somewhat disconcerted when the contents of the barrel were disgorged on the cobbles and Hendriks was unbound sufficiently to stand upright, which, after so long a time crouching, he found great difficulty in doing.

'I assume this gentleman will require other quarters?' said Bouwman.

'Your darkest, deepest dungeon would be good,' Beniamino suggested.

'I would like him made secure, but as comfortable as possible,' I added. 'He is co-operating with us.'

Hendriks was led away, and we ascended to Bouwman's office, and through there to his parlour.

'We will be more comfortable here,' Bouwman told us, and poured us each a cup of wine. 'Now, how can I assist you?'

'I understand that the Stadhouder is expected here tomorrow,' I answered.

'Ye-es,' agreed Bouwman, 'though his movements of late have been somewhat disordered by the excitement.'

'Excitement?'

Bouwman sipped his wine before answering. 'I know that I can trust to your discretion. The Duke of Monmouth has been welcomed here on condition that he made no move to capture the English throne. A number of gentlemen from Scotland and England have urged him to rescue his country from the Catholic designs of King James. Now, I make bold to say that I believe that the Duke is a man of his word, and he would not have made that commitment to the Stadhouder lightly or with no intention of honouring it. However, he is also a man of honour and duty, and it is upon those sentiments that his visitors have played. They have convinced him that he is bound by his birth and status to lead a rebellion, however reluctantly. In view of his previous undertaking, the Duke very properly quitted this court, returned to Brussels and there sold all his goods to finance the undertaking.'

'I knew something of this,' I conceded.

'Indeed. And as a man of sensitivity the Duke would not put the Stadhouder in the position of knowing that a rebellion was being launched from these lands against his uncle and father-in-law.'

These were not two different people. King James was William's uncle and his father-in-law simultaneously.

Bouwman appeared to have difficulty in framing his next remarks to his satisfaction, as if it was not his place to criticise his social superiors. 'Unfortunately, this could be achieved in two ways. He could launch it from somewhere else, or he could do so from here under conditions of secrecy. Knowing the Duke to be a man of integrity, I do not doubt that his intention was to act from Brussels; but his eviction from that city, and the discovery that his forces were being mustered by his lieutenants in our territories, must have left him in an awkward position. I think that he judged that if he kept the Stadhouder in ignorance there would be no risk of embarrassing this country. His Excellency could truthfully say he had no knowledge of the Duke's plans.'

I thought this was very considerate of the Duke, but Beniamino saw a problem.

'But he cannot have supposed that the Stadhouder could ignore the presence of foreign soldiers in his realm?'

'Indeed not; and that is why the Stadhouder has gone himself to see what is going on.'

'To Texel?' I blurted out.

'Where did you hear that?' Bouwman demanded sharply.

Me and my loose tongue! I could hardly say that Princess Mary told me and put her in bad odour with her husband. 'I — er — must have overheard it somewhere.' I tried to change the subject. 'The guards told us he was at Apeldoorn.'

'That is what has been noised abroad for public consumption. If people knew that he had gone to Texel they would wonder why, and then the whole story would come out.'

'Would that be so terrible?'

'Think, Master,' said Beniamino. 'If the Stadhouder goes to a place in the back of beyond like Texel it's hard to imagine a reason for doing so if he doesn't already know the Duke is gathering a fleet there. It would make him look complicit in Monmouth's treason.'

I was shocked. 'Treason is a strong word.'

'What else do you call filling ships with soldiers and invading your own country with the intention of removing the King?'

I had to admit that Beniamino had a point.

Bouwman looked as if he had licked a salt block. 'It's worse than that. We have had word that the Earl of Argyll has already sailed from there for Scotland.'

'Who is this Earl of Argyll?' I asked. Noblemen seemed to be multiplying before me.

'He is a Scottish gentleman,' Bouwman explained.

'The worst kind of adventurer,' Beniamino added. 'King Charles of England deprived him of his estates and he escaped to exile. He seeks to recover his estates now, and knows that as a staunch anti-Catholic he will never be in favour with King James. But if he has sailed for Scotland we must assume that Monmouth is about to sail too. He may only be waiting for Hendriks' report.'

'Why is Argyll going to Scotland if Monmouth is going to England? Wouldn't it make sense for them to invade the same place?'

Beniamino put a brotherly arm round me. 'Bless you, Master, you're a true innocent in such matters. They are invading at the north and south of the country to make James split his army. Fighting on two fronts will tax his generalship.'

'I thought King James was not a great general. Surely he will delegate the fighting to others?'

'Master, for the sake of the Stadhouder's claim to the throne, I hope you're right; for if James leads the fighting himself, he is lost.'

I gulped down the remains of my wine and absentmindedly stuffed a slice of ham in my mouth without remembering to chew, causing me to cough and splutter. Beniamino slapped me hard on the back.

'Thank you,' I wheezed. 'I was distracted. Beniamino, if Monmouth is just waiting for Hendriks' report before sailing, surely the best way to interfere in his plans is not to give him the report.'

'You might think so,' Beniamino answered, 'but I've met the Duke. If I know my man, he will go anyway and try to land at Exeter. And we know if he does that there will be terrible slaughter of his men.'

'I agree,' said Bouwman. 'If he has given his word to attack England simultaneously with Argyll's Scottish invasion he will not tarry. However unpropitious it might be, he will chance his arm.'

'Then you had better go to Monmouth with all speed,' I urged.

'And will you go to Texel to report to the Stadhouder?' said Bouwman.

I had not anticipated that suggestion, and highly unwelcome it was too. I had hoped that we would have handed over our prisoner and I would be on my way back to Leiden by now. The thought of a day — or worse, a night — on horseback appalled me. I wished I had paid more attention in my geography class at school, because all I knew about Texel was that it was a large island at the very north of our country; which meant another confounded ferry. It must be the better part of a hundred miles from The Hague, and given my sense of direction goodness knows where I would end up.

'I think the Master might miss the Stadhouder,' Beniamino chipped in. 'Better that he should stay here and be sure of meeting him.'

Amen to that, I thought. I am not a hedonist, but the idea of a night or two in a soft bed with a warm fire, good food and drink, and the company of an educated man like Bouwman — and possibly Princess Mary — was very enticing.

[Van der Meer has just made a suggestion of the most vulgar kind regarding my motives with respect to the Princess. I had no such intention. First, because I am a priest of the Catholic church and hence sworn to a life of celibacy; and second, because William was the most jealous of husbands and while I had no plans to use my testicles I rather wanted to keep them.]

Beniamino retired to the guardroom to discuss the keeping of our prisoner while Bouwman saw us provided with supper and found rooms for us. I had assumed that Beniamino would want to leave at once but he announced that he would ride faster after a night's sleep. When he said "night" I naïvely assumed he meant all the hours of darkness, and was therefore somewhat disconcerted when he entered my chamber before dawn to take his leave of me.

'What time is it?' I croaked.

'About four. They're saddling the horse so I can be gone at first light. But I couldn't leave without saying goodbye to you.'

Actually, I wouldn't have minded one bit, I thought.

'I doubt we'll meet again, but then I thought that the last time.'

The remembrance that he had now saved my life at least twice made me feel churlish for resenting being woken.

'God go with you,' I said, 'and keep you safe.'

Beniamino slapped me heartily on the back. 'He has so far! I wish you the same, Master. Give my best wishes to the Stadhouder when you see him.' He sat familiarly on the edge of the bed. 'And try to persuade him that you're not cut out for this kind of mission.'

'Believe me, I will.'

If the truth be told, that I was not suited to this work was a self-evident conclusion to anyone who could see what a mess I had made of things.

Beniamino rose to his feet. 'Well, I can't waste the best part of the day talking to you. I must find the Duke.'

I should not have thought that would be too difficult. When all is said and done, people usually remember if they have seen an army marching past, and are able to tell you which way it was headed. If it was like most armies, there would be a company of ravaged women and despoiled barns to mark their passage.

And, just like that, he was gone.

At breakfast I found myself renewing my acquaintance with Princess Mary. She was not eating, having already eaten with her ladies, but came to see me when she heard that I was in the building.

'Please don't rise,' she commanded. 'I had not meant to disturb your breakfast.'

'It is no disturbance, I assure you, madame,' I replied.

'I am delighted to see you returned safely, Master.'

'No more than I am myself.'

She smiled weakly. 'I am concerned about my cousin Monmouth. He intends to contest the throne, you know.'

'So I understand. That must be vexing, given your own better claim.'

She waved away my supposition. 'I care nothing for the throne. What is it but worry and danger? My grandfather was beheaded and there are rumours that my uncle was poisoned.'

If Charles II was poisoned the obvious culprit would surely be her father the King, but it seemed impolite to make that suggestion.

'No, Master, my fear is that he is underprovided for such an undertaking. You have been in England. Did you observe any great support for him?'

'I was not there for long,' I said, hoping that I could avoid actually answering the question. This is a technique that I have learned from a succession of undergraduates who seek to evade the question posed by arguing that they are not in a position to answer the question so it is unfair to ask it.

'I think you are seeking to avoid giving me pain,' said Princess Mary. She was always an intelligent woman.

'I believe he may have some support in London,' I replied, 'but I saw very little evidence of it in Exeter.'

Mary nodded as if her worst fears had been confirmed. 'Thank you,' she said. 'I will pray for him, for I fear I shall never see him again in this world.'

She was right about that.

CHAPTER TWENTY-TWO

Two days later William turned up. After a prolonged period in the saddle he was not in the best of humours. He went first to see his wife, then returned to his private chamber to hear Bouwman's account of what had transpired in his absence before he found time to speak to me.

'Apologies, Master. I had not intended to keep you waiting but the affairs of the nation must come first.' He stared into the fire as if in a grim frame of mind. 'Monmouth is about to depart. He will not hear of any delay because he has engaged himself to invade at the same time as Argyll and would be dishonoured if he did otherwise.'

'Did Beniamino find him, Your Excellency?'

'Well, he found me; and he left soon after to join the Duke's camp. I think we can assume that Monmouth has received his report.'

'I fear that it will make no difference. His enterprise is doomed wherever he lands.'

William kicked a smouldering log into the midst of the fire. 'The best we can hope for is that my plan succeeds and James' army is present in such numbers that the futility of giving battle is clear even to Monmouth. But even if he seeks a truce, why should James grant it when he knows he will win? I fear for him, Mercurius. He is not a bad man, and he is no coward, but he is destined to fail, I'm afraid.'

I could not avoid the subject any longer. 'I am afraid that I too failed, Stadhouder,' I admitted. I recounted how the letter of accreditation had been stolen, and I had suspected Velders but it had transpired that the real villain was Hendriks. 'I am sorry that you were deceived in such a way,' I concluded.

'I wasn't,' claimed William.

'I beg your pardon?'

'I doubted Hendriks but I could not be sure, so I told him that you had the letter. I did not expect him to offer violence, so I am glad that you are unharmed.'

I felt a surge of anger. I had been put at risk, but, more to the point, so had others. 'I am unscathed, but Captain Velders is not.'

William rummaged on his desk for a letter and handed it to me. It was from Van Citters informing him that Velders had finally regained consciousness. He remained feeble and could not walk, but he had been taken into the ambassador's household to recover his strength preparatory to returning home. 'He'll get a good pension, Mercurius, I'll see to that.'

'Hendriks is in the keep here,' I said. 'I stopped Beniamino executing him.'

'I'm glad you did,' said William. 'If anyone is going to have that pleasure it should be me.'

I was uneasy at hearing this. 'I should point out that he has co-operated with me since he was captured, and it is in no small measure due to his co-operation that we have done all we can to avert bloodshed. Without the report that Beniamino took to the Duke he would have attempted to land at an unsuitable port.'

William took this in, but disagreed. 'He's not a fool, Mercurius. When he got to Exeter he would see it was unsuited to his purpose, and would try somewhere else; but he would have forfeited any element of surprise. Well, if I'm not to hang Hendriks, what do you recommend I do to him?'

'He must compensate Velders, of course, but to do that he must remain at liberty. He has a great zeal for the Protestant religion.'

'Then let him serve the church, for I'll not have him in my service,' William replied. The Stadhouder flopped into a chair, which meant that I could sit too. I was suddenly mightily weary. 'Van Citters tells me you have a price on your head in England.'

'Do I?'

I must have brightened up to hear this, because William immediately pricked my pride.

'Don't get excited, Mercurius, it's only five pounds. But you're a fugitive. It may be some time before you can return there.'

'Oh, dear. What a shame,' I lied. For once, my cheeks did not give me away.

It seems that Beniamino had told William all about my time in prison and his rescue, because before I left William gave me a handsome sum in thanks for my work. He also lent me a carriage for the journey back to Leiden, so I was spared any further horse-riding with the attendant indignity such an exploit always seems to lay on me.

Hendriks was given a job in the church as some sort of administrator, half his salary going to Velders for the remainder of his life. As we feared, Monmouth's invasion went badly. Few came to his colours, and his army was routed as he headed towards London. He was captured, tried and executed, as were many of his followers. King James showed absolutely no mercy to his nephew and his adherents. When news reached The Hague of Monmouth's beheading Princess Mary took to her room and remained there for some days in the deepest state of melancholy. I believe that Beniamino survived the battle and escaped by way of Wales, though his fate was uncertain for a while.

As for me, I arrived at Leiden to find that my room had been given to another, and the Rector was obliged to give me a small suite intended for professors. I stowed my bag there, washed myself and went downstairs to the refectory to see if there was any food available. As I entered, Mechtild was wiping a table.

She looked up, threw the cloth down and ran to embrace me. 'Thank God that you are returned safely!' she said.

'Amen to that,' I replied.

She wiped away a tear from her cheek. 'Next time you're sent for, tell that Stadhouder you're not going,' she ordered.

I would love to, I thought, *but it doesn't work like that.*

A NOTE TO THE READER

Dear Reader,

I hope you have enjoyed reading this book. It is, perhaps, more of an adventure than a mystery, but it has its roots in real events.

William of Orange faced a genuine dilemma in 1685. The Duke of Monmouth had promised not to use William's lands as a base for an invasion of England, but King James was trying to keep Monmouth moving to deny him the time and space to set anything in hand. At the same time dispossessed noblemen like Argyll saw a rebellion led by Monmouth as their best hope of recovering their property, and urged him on. William was acutely aware that his wife was heir to the British throne so a successful invasion would damage his prospects too.

The books I used for this story include:

The Later Stuarts 1660–1714 (2nd edition), by Sir George Clark

The Last Royal Rebel, by Anna Keay

Dutch Ships in Tropical Waters, by Robert Parthesius

The History of the London Water Industry, 1580–1820, by Leslie Tomory

James II, by David Womersley.

Of course, this is not a history book and I have to take a few liberties with the facts to craft a believable story, but I hope those who know the history well will not think I have twisted it too much.

A number of readers have expressed concern for poor Van der Meer. I wish I had his patience, but I am very grateful for his diligence in transcribing Mercurius' adventures.

If you have enjoyed this novel, I'd be really grateful if you would leave a review on **Amazon** and **Goodreads**. I love to hear from readers, so please keep in touch through **Facebook** or **Twitter**, or leave a message on my **website**.

Dank je wel!

Graham Brack

Sapere Books is an exciting new publisher of brilliant fiction and popular history.

To find out more about our latest releases and our monthly bargain books visit our website: **saperebooks.com**